THE BASTARD PRINCE

The Bastard Prince
Captured Hearts 2.5
By Megan Derr

Published by Megan Derr

Edited by Michelle McDonough and Samantha Derr
Cover art by Aisha Akeju

Third Edition March 2020
Copyright © 2020 by Megan Derr
First Edition published January 2010 by Less Than Three Press

Printed in the United States of America

THE BASTARD PRINCE

CAPTURED HEARTS 2.5

MEGAN DERR

⊕NE

Reyes scowled in annoyance at the flowers on his desk. They were, as always, exquisite. Roses this week: an enormous bouquet of them, ranging in color from brilliant orange through blushing pink and fading finally to creamy yellow, with a host of shades in between. Beautiful and perfectly arranged in a vase of delicate pale blue crystal.

He set his ledgers and portfolios down on his desk, ignoring the roses, and moved to open the drapes. The office flooded with weak, hazy light, bringing a little bit of life to the golden woods, the jeweled green and gold tones of the furnishings, the myriad colors in the costly woven rug.

A soft knock up on the door drew Reyes's attention, and he turned to smile in greeting at the elderly woman who bustled in amidst a clatter of dishes and the smell of coffee, fresh bread, cinnamon, and apples. "Good morning, Maggie."

"Good morning, Master O'Bannon," Maggie replied, steadfast in her refusal to lessen her formality even to 'Master Reyes.' "Cook made cinnamon bread this morning, and I knew you'd be wanting that, so I made sure there was extra on the plate. There's also the apple spread to go with, and I kept that fool boy Josh from making the coffee this morning."

Reyes adjusted the spectacles on his nose as he set a stack of envelopes and papers at his seat at the table. He squeezed her hand gently after she had set the tray down and fussed with it until satisfied. "Thank you, Maggie. Perfect, as always."

She flushed, but only fussed with her apron then curtsied politely. "Enjoy your breakfast, Master O'Bannon. Call if you've need. G'day, now."

"Good day, Maggie."

When she had gone, he took up the coffee pot and poured himself a cup, sipping it as he began to go through the early morning post. He frowned in concern as he read the first letter and reached out to tug on the green bell pull. A couple of minutes later, a young man appeared with barely a sound. He was dressed in the forest green uniform of the royal military, the stripes on his chest identifying him as a sergeant.

"Tell the captain to come to me at his earliest convenience."

"Yes, sir," the soldier replied and left as quietly as he had arrived.

Setting the letter aside, Reyes moved on to the next, making a note of it in his portfolio before setting it aside in a separate pile. Then it was on to the next, and he worked steadily through the mound of correspondence.

About halfway through the stack, he paused to refill his cup and pour a second. To that one he added cream, then set it before the empty chair across the table from his own.

Returning to the letters, he opened one bearing the moon and cross sigil of the Southern Monastery; it was rare to receive correspondence from that little corner of the kingdom. Reading the letter, Reyes's eyebrows immediately shot up in surprise, then drew together in concern. Picking up the first letter, which bore the marks of the Northern Treasury, he compared the two.

He set them to the side and reached for the bell

pulls once more, this time ringing the green, followed by the gray. A couple of minutes later, the young soldier appeared again, as silently as ever. Seconds later, another young man entered, dressed in the pale gray robes of an acolyte.

"Tell the captain I need to see him at once," Reyes told the soldier. To the priest, he said," Tell His Grace I request his immediate presence."

"Yes, sir," the men chorused and turned to depart—only to stumble to a frantic halt and tumble over in hasty, clumsy bows. "Good Morning, Your Majesty."

"Good morning," King Rhoten greeted sleepily, patting them absently on the shoulder, trying and failing to stifle a yawn. He sat down as the two men finally departed and smiled. "Good morning, Reyes."

"Good morning, Majesty," Reyes replied and handed him the two letters of concern. "Two attacks in completely different parts of the country but remarkably similar. Two groups of bandits, ten to twelve in number, attacked the Northern Treasury and the Southern Monastery. In each case, the robbers were successfully routed, but the attacks showed careful planning and inside knowledge."

Rhoten frowned and quickly read through the letters, finishing his coffee quickly. Setting the cup aside, he read through the letters a second time, then a third.

Reyes quietly prepared him a fresh cup of coffee, and then prepared two more, one made black, the other with cream and sugar. These he put at two of the four remaining seats. There was a brisk knock upon the door just as he finished.

It opened to admit two older men, both in their early forties. The first was dressed in brown breeches and boots and a handsomely cut forest green jacket with the marks of Captain of the Guard upon his breast and forearms. His nut-brown hair was cut short and neat, only barely touched with silver, drawing attention to the sharp, clear color of his bright blue eyes. One hand rested with the ease of a lifetime upon the hilt of the sword at his hip, an emerald gleaming in its pommel.

Beside him was the High Priest, the mirror image of the captain, save that his hair was a bit longer, less severely cut, and he was dressed in the flowing pale gray robes of the priesthood. On his chest, over his heart, was stitched the moon and tri-star crest of the royal priests. Directly opposite it was the runic sun and moon crest that designated his rank.

Twins, and extremely close—so close that their drastically different callings had not managed to tear them apart even the slightest. If anything, their relationship had helped to mend a long-standing breach between the military and the priests.

"Sit down, please," Reyes said, motioning. "I apologize for bothering the both of you so early."

"Never a bother, Your Majesty, Reyes," the High Priest replied, smiling as he took his seat and immediately sipped at his black coffee. "Especially since you always have the best coffee in the palace. Alas, I can tell this is not a social visit. What is wrong?"

Rhoten handed them the letters. "Erices, Breit, we've trouble brewing, I think. Two attacks, exactly alike, completely opposite corners of the kingdom. These letters would have come with full urgency, save that each had no way of knowing their attack was a copy of the other."

Erices drank most of his sweet, cream-heavy coffee as he read quickly but thoroughly. Finished, he handed them to his brother. "Two of our most fortified keeps. The attacks, if accurately described, have the feel of testing for weaknesses, feeling out an enemy."

"I agree," Rhoten said.

"Yes," Breit said, setting the letters down after he had read them. "To what purpose, however? Both attacks failed; I hope that works to our favor. The treasury and monastery have only the strength of their fortifications in common. Both were built by the same man, I believe."

"I am more troubled by the fact they had inside help," Erices said, sipping the rest of his coffee, nodding briefly in thanks as Reyes fixed his second cup. "The time of year is peculiar as well—we are only weeks away from Extended Night. Granted, more to the south they will not suffer it as extremely as we do here, but in the north it will be even worse. The robbers could not manage further attacks without at least three mages of respectable ability. Contracting them would bring an exorbitant price."

Reyes nodded absently at this, though he had no real place in the conversation. He was the royal secretary, and no one present would take it amiss if he offered his opinion, but he preferred to remain silent, keep the coffee and food to hand, and make notes of everything while they talked.

He made careful note of the magic, adding his own to see it looked into. An eye was always kept on the unlicensed lots—more of an eye than anyone realized. If someone was attempting to coordinate an attack this time of year, they would require mages to provide vast quantities of light and heat. In two weeks' time, Extended Night would fall, and they would not see true cycles of night and day again for three months. So deep into winter, mages were already completely occupied maintaining the heating amongst the cities and villages. One hundred alone maintained the royal palace, holding back temperatures that would freeze a man in the time it took to draw breath.

Such an operation, if the attacks continued—which was not an impossibility—would require several unlicensed mages or several licensed mages acting without authority.

He refilled Rhoten's coffee and added cream, glancing surreptitiously at the men gathered around the table. Three of the most powerful mages in the world sat here, discussing matters of state and security with the calm most people showed for weather and fashion and balls.

Rhoten, of course, had the most powerful special magic in the country—a very simple, straightforward ability to destroy things. Being so close to him, Reyes was quite familiar with his ability to destroy anything from a book to a building with the proper amount of focus and energy.

The Horn twins were as notorious for their magical prowess as they were for being so similar in appearance and so different in manner. They had held royal licenses for nearly as long as they had worked in the palace. Both had high level mastery of elemental magic—especially the fire magic so crucial to survival in their brutally cold climate. Erices was also a healer, while Breit had carried his elemental skills to an even greater level that made him the best in the country.

"There is a chance, however thin and unlikely," Breit said, "that this is not as bad as we are already preparing for it to be. Then again, Galand has been too quiet of late."

"Agreed," Rhoten said. "I think we will keep this affair between us, and as quiet as possible, until we know better the exact nature of what we are or are not facing. Breit, you are departing soon to visit the monastery anyway, are you not?"

Breit nodded. "I was to leave tomorrow

morning."

Rhoten smiled. "I think your brother feels in need of a break before Extended Night settles upon us and so has decided to accompany you. I am certain it will not look amiss if he wants to spend his time exploring and riding and otherwise being a terrible distraction to his brother, who is kind enough to indulge him and go about with him."

The brothers smiled together, two slow, feral smiles that only hinted as to why one did so well as Captain of the Guard and the other had so quickly climbed the ranks to High Priest. "Yes, Majesty," Erices replied. "If I may ask, though, who do you intend to send to investigate the Northern Treasury?"

For reply, the king only glanced over Reyes's shoulder to the vibrant roses set on the corner of his desk.

Realizing the direction of his gaze, Reyes rolled his eyes and barely stifled a groan. Rhoten chuckled at his reaction and said, "It has been some time since my falcon has stretched his wings. He has been confined and restless since breaking his leg, and that is now well-healed. I think I will remove his jesses. Reyes, summon him, and I think we will need more coffee."

Though he had already been aware of the need for more coffee, Reyes only murmured a quiet "Yes, Majesty" and reached out to tug on the blue bell pull. "Maggie," he said when she promptly appeared. "More coffee, if you please, and see that someone fetches Lord Hess. Thank you."

"Yes, sir. Majesty. Your lordships." Maggie curtsied and was gone.

Erices smirked at Reyes. "Still being courted, Reyes? I was with the gatehouse guards this morning when Kinnaird returned from his weekly trip with those roses. He looked most pleased with himself."

"I see," Reyes said, refusing to react to the teasing. Why everyone found it amusing instead of troubling, he did not know—even Kinnaird's rather colorful family history did not excuse his behavior.

The men all laughed and smiled quietly, then subsided into the food and coffee Maggie brought and more general talk while they waited for Kinnaird to arrive.

A few minutes later the familiar, quick four knocks came at the door, and it opened to admit Lord Kinnaird Hess, eleventh Duke of Keyes. Like the roses, he was as exquisite as ever. His hair was a fascinating combination of distinct shades of gold, brown, and red. His eyes were a brilliant amber, razor sharp, and set in features that were just as severe but strangely beautiful for it.

It was little surprise, really, that his family possessed one of the rarest and most coveted magical abilities in the country, one important enough that eleven generations ago, the crown had bestowed upon his ancestors a duchy.

Most magic could be universally learned. In the harsh, cold climate in which they lived, every mage learned at least basic elemental magic and a little healing. There was, however, a small collection of special magical abilities that were exclusive to the individual families that possessed them. In all the kingdom, there were nine families that possessed the ability to shift form. Of these, one family and one alone could transform into a creature with wings. It suited Kinnaird, naturally, that he could turn into a falcon.

"Your Majesty," Kinnaird said, sweeping them an elegant bow. He was dressed in brown breeches, cream-colored clocked stockings with a rune-and-feather image, gold-buckled court shoes, and a handsome jacket of dark, tawny superfine that matched exactly every shade of his fascinating hair, further accented with touches of cream lace and tiny topazes. "Captain, Lord High Priest. Reyes, you are as breathtaking as ever. The roses hardly do you justice, I do apologize for them."

Reyes rolled his eyes. "Good morning, Your Grace. Thank you for the flowers. Would you care to join us?"

Chuckling, Kinnaird sat down in the chair next to Reyes and helped himself to coffee before Reyes could fix it for him—and he could not prepare it beforehand because Kinnaird seemed to drink it a different way every single time. Reyes could not understand why Kinnaird always made a point of never letting Reyes assist or serve him. No doubt it was purely for purposes of vexation.

Sipping his own coffee, Reyes sat quietly while the others brought Kinnaird up to date on everything, and Erices handed him the letters.

Kinnaird grimaced as he finished, setting them aside after only one read-through. "These letters are terrible. No real details as to how the robbers attacked or what particularly causes them to think there was inside information. They do not discuss the robbers at all really, which would have saved us a great deal of time and speculation. There are all manner of details they should have noted and should have included— language, appearance, manner, weaponry, clothing, jewelry, methods of attack. I do not suppose they have at least bothered to keep one or two alive?"

Erices grunted. "The treasury will have kept a couple; they know the sorts of things such prisoners can reveal when properly persuaded. The monastery, however, does not really have anywhere to keep someone effectively confined. They would have killed them all rather than risk further trouble."

Kinnaird looked at the letters in disgust. "I shall be off at once, then. Should anyone ask, I have decided to take myself off to my private hot springs for a few days. Care to join me there, my dear?" he asked Reyes.

"No, but thank you, Your Grace."

The king laughed. "Splendid. All parties are to keep me well informed. Send careful letters, of course."

"Of course," Breit repeated and stood up. "Shall we then, Eri? We've much to prepare if you are to come with me. Majesty, thank you for breakfast." Nodding, bowing, the brothers departed.

Standing up, eyes bright with mirth, mouth curved in a smirk, the king said, "I shall work in my office for a bit, I think. Reyes, come find me in an hour or so." Then he was gone, the door to his inner office clicking shut quietly behind him.

Leaving Reyes alone with Kinnaird. "Should you not be going, Your Grace?"

Kinnaird somehow had managed to move his chair closer without Reyes actually seeing him do it. "Did you like the roses?" he asked and reached out briefly to dust Reyes's cheek with his knuckles.

Reyes jerked away, trying to ignore the warm touch, the way Kinnaird smelled like silk and peppermint oil. It was always so surprisingly cool a scent for a man of such warm colors, but the sharpness of it suited him. "The flowers are beautiful, Your Grace. As always, I thank you. Also as always, I remind you that you should not be giving flowers to me, especially such costly ones, and especially when you are being pressured to marry."

"I will give flowers where I choose and marry when and where I choose. You like to continually overlook that I am the king's falcon, and I have his permission to press my suit where I like. My sister married well and has been blessed with five children.

By the grace of sun and moon, three of them are daughters. My line does not want for heirs."

"I am a secretary, and you are a duke, and one of the oldest titles in the country. Press your suit elsewhere, Your Grace, for I do, and shall continue to, refuse it."

Kinnaird only smiled and drew back slightly. He shrugged one elegant shoulder and said, "If I were inclined to give up so easily, my dear, I would not be the king's falcon. However, if you like, we can wait to continue this conversation upon my return. Rest assured, however, I shall not give up."

Reyes had no intention of continuing the conversation anytime. "Sun and moon shine upon your journey, Your Grace."

"Thank you." Kinnaird stood up, and Reyes turned away, back to the work that had lain neglected while the meeting carried on. "Oh, just one more thing."

"Hmm?" Reyes asked absently, half-turning in his seat and looking up—

To be met by Kinnaird's mouth, warm and sudden and flavored of coffee and apples and cinnamon. Reyes pulled away, but far too late to hide the fact that, for a few seconds, he had responded to and returned the kiss.

"For luck," Kinnaird said with a wink, backing well out of range of any swing Reyes might take. "Think happy thoughts to bring me home to you, should I become lost in the snow." Reyes rolled his eyes at the folk tale reference. Kinnaird smiled and blew him a kiss from the doorway. "Sun and moon watch over you. Farewell."

Reyes let out a frustrated breath, scrubbing at his lips to banish the taste and feel of Kinnaird, but the memories lingered in his mind, hot and bright. No amount of scrubbing would banish those.

Grimacing, he gathered up the post and abandoned the table in favor of his desk. Barely had the sun bells rung, signaling the formal start of day than he was inundated with people needing to see the king, needing appointments made, needing papers signed, projects approved, and crises solved.

He handled it all well, with all the skill and ability that had swiftly moved him from a mere general secretary to secondary secretary of the Marquis of White to the minor secretary of the king to the king's primary secretary, and finally to the king's *only* secretary, when the king decided that Reyes was all he needed and would tolerate.

When the mid-bells rang, Reyes told the guards outside the office to ban entrance for the next hour. Alone at last, the king still out riding with a couple of his favorite advisors, Reyes took a much-needed break. Crossing the room, he pushed a hidden button that opened a secret door, which in turn led to a small room.

Closing the door firmly behind him and locking it, Reyes poured water from a blue china pitcher into the matching bowl. Then he held his hand over the water and willed it to heat. The surge of magic was warm as it raced through his blood, flushing his skin slightly. In the bowl, steam began to rise lazily from the water.

Relaxing his power, Reyes stripped off his jacket, shirt, and undershirt, hanging them on nearby hooks. Then he reached for the soap in a small china dish. It smelled faintly of lavender, and he breathed it in, reminded briefly of home, before picking up a washing rag and scrubbing himself down. Clean and dried, he felt much refreshed as he put his clothes back on.

He frowned at the drying towel then glanced up

at his reflection in the looking glass above the wash basin. His hair was becoming intolerable, taking in the dark brown strands that lightened to dark gold at the tips. He would have to tend to it tonight.

Setting the matter aside for the time being, he set down the drying towel and adjusted his clothing. He smoothed down the soft, dark blue velvet of his jacket, the silk of his silver and blue striped waistcoat, tweaking the crisp, white lace cuffs to fall just so. Finally he settled his silver-rimmed spectacles, attached by delicate chain to his waistcoat, on his nose.

He lingered a couple of minutes more, helplessly and pathetically drawn to his reflection, wondering what someone like Kinnaird saw in him, what made him claim he cared. If he—

Cutting the thought off, Reyes left the freshening up room and returned to his office proper, smiling when he saw that Maggie had already come and gone, leaving a fine lunch spread out on the table.

Sitting down, Reyes dug in with relish, carefully avoiding thinking about either work or Kinnaird.

Two

Kinnaird shifted in the forest, well away from the city. People envied his magic, had been willing to do a variety of things on the chance there might actually be a way to learn it, but all were uncomfortable with actually watching the change.

At least his great-great-great grandfather had mastered the art of keeping the clothes, even if Kinnaird did not entirely grasp the workings.

He shivered in the brutal cold and raised his heat shields another increment. Snow and ice, as far as the eye could see. This time of year it was perpetually dark, with never anything more than a hint of light, the sun always hovering just out of sight when it rose. The moon offered more light this time of year, reflecting off the snow.

As ever, the unending fields and forests of white brought to mind the old folk tale of the lost prince—one of many his mother had loved to tell him. Once upon a time, it went, a prince was called off to war. He dutifully went, reluctantly leaving behind his beautiful, faithful bride. The years passed and passed, until at last the war ended and the prince was permitted to return home.

However, on the journey home, the prince became lost in a terrible winter storm, and this in the heart of Extended Night, when there was no hope for ever seeing the sun. He tried to find his way, but only became more and more lost, until he grew tired and despaired of ever finding home.

But, lo, just as he began to succumb to the cold, he heard a voice. In whispers and snatches at first, but with increasing strength and volume, until he realized that it was his bride's thoughts he could hear.

He followed her thoughts, used them to guide himself home, until at last he fell into her arms. She was even more faithful and more beautiful than when he had left her, waiting patiently for his return. They were married shortly thereafter, and for the rest of their lives the prince and his princess shared thoughts.

The tale was often cited as a whimsical founding tale of the creation of a legendary special magic. No one living or in recent history could use mind-share magic. Those who history said could were mostly legend, and their abilities great exaggeration.

Except… sometimes Kinnaird suspected Erices and Breit could do it. Something about those two, the looks they exchanged, the way they sometimes knew things even though they had not seen one another the whole day… He rather thought they had a few secrets to which even the king was not privy.

He shook snow from his dark russet cloak, scrubbed it from his hair with his thick-gloved hands, before pulling up the deep, fur-lined hood and securing it in place against the wind. Then he trudged on, making his way with relative speed toward the nearby city.

Feyestone was the northernmost city in the country, several days hard travel in good weather from the next city, which was one of the smaller harbor cities. Remote and north as it was, Feyestone spent much of its time in absolute day or absolute night. Getting to it was no easy task, and not a trip foreigners were typically inclined to make.

Except neighboring Galand, but they had

arduous, life-stealing mountain cities enough of their own. They were also greedy, though, and well-positioned to manage coordinated attacks at opposite ends of Elamas.

Feyestone was a handsome city, if remote and severe and somewhat old-fashioned. Everything, from the high walls of the outer and inner curtains, to all the buildings inside, was carved from the dark, gray, nearly indestructible rock that gave the city its name. It was also extremely good at keeping in heat, a necessity in a place that seldom ceased to endure snow and ice.

At the farthest end of the city was the original keep, built into the mountain itself. From the keep, over the years and generations, the castle had expanded into a full-blown city. It had been its own province once, like most of the cities scattered across the frozen continent. At the end of Queen Basden's war, she had succeeded in uniting the choicest pieces of the continent under her crown, leaving the rest of the land eventually to break up into four other countries.

Elamas, still ruled by the descendants of Basden, was called the Diamond of the North for its diamond-like shape and its lucrative trading industry—trade that was the lifeblood of Elamas, after the magic that made living there possible.

Bordering Elamas were the countries of Galand and Lesed. Lesed, at present, was locked in a civil war. The borders had been completely closed for nearly a year, with little to no communication from the outside. At the crown's insistence, Elamas had stayed out of the matter.

Galand, however… Yes, Galand fit the part for outside help. Kinnaird would bet his title on it. They had never been satisfied with their land-locked status, how heavily they relied on the countries surrounding them, on the trade agreements they were constantly seeking to improve, forever demanding renegotiations of the trade agreements and tariffs, and continental history was rife with failed coups as they tried to take over one of the coastline countries.

So he wondered if they might not be up to something similar now. It was a bit of a leap, given how little was known of the situation, but what better time to attack than during Extended Night?

It was the most taxing, most dangerous time of year for the country—and for the mages especially. Not only were they expending great amounts of time and energy to keep everyone safely warm, they also had to work to provide additional light where mere candles and lanterns would not suffice. If someone wanted to stage a coup, finding a way to do it during Extended Night would be a sound strategic move.

Reaching the city gates, shaking off snow, Kinnaird pounded on the small gatehouse door built into the heavy iron-plated door of the outer gate. "Open in the name of the King!"

Movement caught his eyes, and he looked up into the snow at the figure that leaned out from one of the towers of the gatehouse. "Who goes there, making demands in the name of the King?"

"Kinnaird Hess, Duke of Keyes."

"Guess you couldn't lie about that, eh?" the guard called down. "In a moment, Your Grace."

Kinnaird rolled his eyes at the entirely too-casual behavior. If the whole lot behaved in such fashion, it was little wonder robbers had gained access to the city. He stood patiently, listening as the guards on the other side unlocked the door. Finally it opened, and a soldier with pale hair and dark eyes snapped him a salute then swept an elegant bow. "Your Grace, welcome to Feyestone. We are honored by your presence."

"Thank you," Kinnaird replied, smiling at the small group that had assembled. "I am honored to be here. Who is in charge, and where might I find him?" He already knew that Lord Marland was the Baron of Feyestone, but locals liked to be asked, especially by people of importance.

The pale-haired soldier replied, "Technically, Your Grace, that will be Lord Marland. He'll be in the old district round about this time, at a tavern called the Lost Cave. You can't miss it if you just continue straight on all the way down this road toward the keep. But you'll also be wanting a word with Steward Tamark, and he'll be at the keep proper this time of night."

"Thank you," Kinnaird said again, and nodded politely when they bowed, ignoring the whispers that sprang up in his wake. He walked briskly through the quiet streets, absently reaching out to feel the heat shields that kept back the deadly cold and the heavily falling snow, while simultaneously keeping lanterns lit to beat back the relentless dark. Catching hold of the intricate magic weaving, he threaded his own power into it, lending it to the shields for the duration of his stay.

A handful of the mages who felt the change reached out gentle pulses, signaling their thanks. The more in the weaving, the less the strain on all involved in it. He acknowledged the thanks with a gentle pulse of his own then returned his full attention to the tavern now coming into view.

The Lost Cave was about what he would expect of a tavern in this place. Of respectable size, run-down but clean, warm and crowded, smelling heavily of people and sweat and alcohol. He stepped inside but kept his hood up, acknowledging the barkeep's nod of greeting with a hand motion.

Wishing he could afford to stop and eat first, Kinnaird glanced around for the baron, but his eyes were caught by a flash of wavy, dark brown hair.

It was not Reyes, of course, but the hair was markedly similar in length and color. A pity that Reyes kept his shoulder-length hair so tightly braided.

Reyes…

Kinnaird stifled a sigh, and for what seemed the thousandth time, reminded himself it had taken his father seven years to finally marry his mother. Still, courting the king's secretary should be a fair sight easier than wooing an actress.

He thought the flowers might be working in their way. Stealing that kiss had probably not been the wisest idea, but he had not been able to help himself— and he did want Reyes to be forced to acknowledge that Kinnaird was in earnest. Kinnaird had been fascinated with the lanky, pretty, hard-working, and kind Reyes from the moment he had first seen him in the general offices. He had not approached Reyes then, but his obsession had drawn the attention of White, who had taken on Reyes as one of his own secretaries.

Eventually, Rhoten had stolen him away. It was his relationship with Rhoten that Kinnaird had always most admired about Reyes. Anyone else would have, and had, abused the powerful position shamelessly. It had added still more difficulties to Rhoten's already difficult life. Reyes, though, clearly regarded Rhoten with affection, saw him as more than a crown. Since terminating everyone else and keeping only Reyes as his secretary, Rhoten had been much happier. He practically doted on Reyes, perhaps in lieu of the fact he had never had a son, only his daughter, sickly, cold, and distant, generally preferring to be anywhere but home.

Now, if he could just get Reyes to accept his

suit, Kinnaird's own life would be practically perfect.

The brown-haired man who had briefly distracted him laughed, and his laugh was so grating and obnoxious and wrong, any hint of Reyes in him was immediately dispelled.

He returned to the task at hand and finally spotted a man who had to be Lord Marland in a dark corner, a wench spread across his thighs and clinging shamelessly to his shoulders in open invitation. If not for the layers of clothes between them, she would no doubt be riding his cock right there in plain sight.

Kinnaird pushed back his hood and assumed a mantle of haughty disdain as he reached the table. He looked down his nose at the drunk, crude Marland. No wonder he was buried all the way out here in this land that sun and moon barely remembered. "Pardon me," he said coolly, flicking the wench a cold, dismissive glance before leveling his eyes on Marland. Like so many others, he wilted beneath Kinnaird's direct gaze. "You are Lord Marland?"

"Who are you?" Marland demanded.

In reply, Kinnaird reached into his jacket and extracted a leather card case, sliding out one calling card and presenting it. Upon reading it, Marland blanched and tried all in one motion to shove the wench off his lap, stand up, and re-lace his open trousers.

Kinnaird turned politely away to give the baron a moment to recover himself and to spare himself the sight of the oaf's cock.

"Your Grace," Marland finally said. He extended a hand as Kinnaird turned around again. Kinnaird ignored it, and finally the baron dropped his hand back to his side. He gestured they should speak outside and took his things as the barkeep held them out then led the way outside. "What can I do for you, Your Grace? Strange to see one of your esteemed sort all the way out here."

"I have come to further investigate the attempted robbery which occurred several days past," Kinnaird replied.

"Uh— We wrote the letter, not much more—"

Kinnaird cut him off with a motion, disgusted. "Where can I find Steward Tamark?" he asked, mostly to see if Marland even knew that much. He could already tell that it wasn't Marland who kept the city functioning.

"Keep," Marland muttered, looking much as if he knew all too well the trouble he was officially in. "I can show—"

"I would hate to keep you away from your rutting and drinking any longer," Kinnaird said. "Good night, my lord."

"Your Grace."

Turning away, Kinnaird resumed his walk, quickly rising up a steep, cobblestone incline to the pavilion of Feyestone Keep. The old castle had ceased to be used much in that capacity. Instead, it had become the repository for much of the kingdom's treasures and wealth. So difficult to reach, it was perfect for the task of safeguarding valuable property of the kingdom. Should the worst ever come to pass, the crown could flee to Feyestone to make a last stand with all that was necessary to starting and maintaining the country safe within the secret hollows and caves of the mountain into which Feyestone was built.

When he approached the doors to the keep, he was momentarily startled when the guards bowed and greeted him, "Your Grace. Welcome to Feyestone Keep."

"Thank you," Kinnaird replied. The men pulled open the heavy doors made from sturdy wood and plated with iron strips spaced roughly three finger widths apart. He strode into the Great Hall, doors closing shut with a crashing echo behind him.

Three long tables with benches filled most of the hall with a shorter one at the head of them all and chairs set behind it, their backs to the great roaring fireplace.

A man sat at one of the long tables, close to the fire. He lifted an arm in greeting. "Ho, Your Grace. Care for a bit of food, some wine perhaps?"

"Both would be most welcome," Kinnaird replied, and strode down the enormous hall. It was well cared for, clean and orderly, with fine tapestries to cover the windows and banners of past lords hanging from the high beams. The roaring fire bathed the nearest portion of the room in warm light and banished the worst of the dark in all but the farthest corners.

Sitting down, he returned the friendly smile the man across from him extended. The man's face bore the lines and scars of a life spent in the hard lands. Handsome, not yet forty. Dark green eyes, light blond hair, the cut of it soldier short.

"I'd shake hands, Your Grace, but my hands are more than a bit of a mess right now," the man said, smiling. "But do help yourself, if you are so inclined. There's food aplenty, and I've Bale fetching more wine."

"Thank you," Kinnaird replied, mood already vastly improved. Removing his cloak and gloves, setting them aside on an empty table, he sat down and began to help himself to the food. "You must be Steward Tamark."

"Yes, Your Grace, that would be me," Tamark replied. "I can see you met Lord Marland. I am sorry you had so unworthy a welcome."

"This food is all the welcome I require," Kinnaird said. "It is delicious, especially after a hard day's travel. So explain that oaf to me."

Tamark shrugged. "His line owns the land, by the grace of sun and moon and king. We just try to keep him in the taverns and out of our way as much as possible. I suppose you've come about the attack eight days ago. Ah, here is the wine, thank you, Bale." He poured wine for both of them, and Kinnaird was surprised to see both that Bale was the man from the gate and that he looked like a younger version of Tamark.

"This must be your son," he said with a smile.

"Yes," Tamark said with a proud smile. "He came straight to me himself to say that you had come. My eldest, turned eighteen just three days ago. I've another, fifteen in a couple of months, around here somewhere. They're good lads."

"I do not doubt it," Kinnaird replied, meaning it. "Your wife must be proud of all her men."

"She was," Tamark replied, smiling briefly, sadly. "She died three years ago on a hunting trip, but she was proud of her family."

Kinnaird nodded and said only, "I am sorry you lost her."

"Thank you," Tamark said and drank his wine, and Kinnaird went back to his inspection.

Rather than the more modern court style clothing Kinnaird wore, Tamark was dressed in an old-fashioned tunic, cut sleeveless, made of sturdy dark green fabric, trimmed in a dark yellow-gold, the moon, sun, and sword sigil of the royal army emblazoned on his chest in silver and gold thread. The long sleeves of his undercoat were rolled up, revealing a tattoo on his right forearm of the runic symbols for fire and ice.

It also showed his license, a gold first class band set with the various permit sigils, the king's official seal—and a ruby that surprised Kinnaird. "You're a flame master?" he asked, surprised. A master was a mage who had chosen to focus on one particular kind of magic, to the exclusion of practically everything else. Tamark, being a flame master, would have mastered the use of fire magic as far as it was physically possible to go without killing himself. He was no one to be trifled with.

"Yes," Tamark replied, smiling. "They have tried to lure me to Basden several times, but my family has always served as Steward of Feyestone. I will not be the one to break that tradition, not lightly anyway."

Kinnaird nodded. "It is true the capital could always use more good men, especially of your skill, but I would not leave were I you."

Tamark's smile widened, and he drank his wine. "So why did His Majesty send his noble falcon to investigate our little attack? Though troublesome, we have dealt with such things before and dealt with this one well enough. It hardly seems worth Your Grace's time."

"Can I trust you to keep a confidence?" Kinnaird asked.

"Yes, Your Grace."

Kinnaird took a swallow of his own wine—it was good, red and raw, rich in body and flavor—Kinnaird explained the letters, the double attack, their suspicions. When he finished, Tamark poured them more wine and said only, "We kept three of them alive. Would Your Grace like to see them now? We have been leaving them to suffer for the past several days. Two of them are not accustomed to the weather. I think they must come from much further south, where the temperature is kinder." He sneered his opinion of this.

Kinnaird agreed wholeheartedly. His duties had taken him across the world, and it still dumbfounded him how soft people could be about the weather. The slightest bit of cold and they were wasting wood and magic to stay ridiculously hot. Sun and moon, he had hated the countries that never stopped being hot the most.

"No," he said in reply to Tamark's question. "Tomorrow is soon enough for that. Tell me the full of what happened, by your pleasure."

"Of course, Your Grace," Tamark replied, as the evening holy bells began to ring. The bell tower must be close, given the way the sound reverberated through the great hall. It was definitely late, if the evening holy bells were ringing. He could not wait to find his bed, but he made himself focus as Tamark continued, "Eight days ago it was, now. The school end bells had only just rung, and I was waiting for the half-mark bells to ring so I could take a break. There was an uproar from the back sections, where the castle gives way to the mountain. At the same time, there was an outcry from the southeast corner of the outer curtain, flares of magic that knocked the heat shield hard. We barely managed to keep it up. That was not a pleasant moment.

"By the time we got out there, they had gotten over the outer curtain and were making quick work of scaling the inner curtain. If we had been any slower to react, they would have gotten into the keep proper. They had at least five magic users, of a skill to possess at least second-grade licenses, but I doubt any of them were registered. Didn't speak beyond cries and grunts, that sort of thing. Could have been from any of the five kingdoms, really. The ones stewing have yet to talk. They're very quiet; it's almost impressive.

"Anyway, they normally would not have been able to get inside so easily, but they knew of two weaknesses that should not have been known by outsiders. One, the section of the curtains they attacked had recently been badly damaged by a careless apprentice who should not have been anywhere near the curtains. We were waiting for the masons to finish up another project; it was only damaged a week and a half. Unfortunately, several people knew of that particular damage, so anyone could have slipped it to a stranger after a few drinks."

"Unfortunate," Kinnaird said.

"Yes," Tamark replied slowly and finished his wine. "However, no one but I and four others knew of recent damage to some of the cave rooms. One of them collapsed recently, opening up access to the outside. We put up shields, but the unlicensed mages managed to tear them down and seriously injured two of my mages in the process. They're still asleep." He shrugged. "They were doing rounds when it collapsed and reported directly to me. The two mages could not have told anyone, so that leaves the soldiers. They are currently confined to quarters and under guard."

"How did you manage to stop both attacks?"

"I took the curtains. My second managed the men who came up through the caves. We were very lucky, by grace of sun and moon."

Kinnaird's brows went up. "It seems to me security for the Northern Treasury leaves something to be desired."

Tamark grunted. "Don't I know it. I manage as best I can. I control the military, watch over the city, the mages. I keep it running and plunk Lord Marland down long enough to scrawl his name on bits of paper whenever it's necessary. But I can only do so much, especially when he is never around to have my back. What kind of discipline can you expect to maintain when the man in charge is off drinking and fucking anything in a skirt?"

"I understand," Kinnaird said, and made careful

note of all he was going to tell Rhoten upon his return. It was reprehensible that such negligence had gone so long unnoticed. "So it would seem someone is giving away entirely too much information to strangers, and there is no telling what else this someone has let slip."

"Right. Did all too fine a job on this attack, and it definitely had the feel of testing. They'll make another, stronger attack sometime in the next month, I'll wager my place as Steward on it. The mages are braced for it, at least. It scared all of us right proper, how close we came to losing the heat shields."

Kinnaird nodded. "And the good baron is out carousing; I can see he learned a valuable lesson."

Tamark shrugged. "It is what it is, by will of sun and moon. We have learned to endure him and manage without him. At least he stays out of my way. Hopefully his son will someday show more sense."

Nodding, Kinnaird finished his wine and pushed his plate and cup away. "I thank you for the food. I do not suppose I could trouble you for a bed?"

"The solar is readied," Tamark replied, and rang a bell next to his hand. "His lordship never uses it. He prefers to live in his house in the city. Our old castle does not suit him." He did not express his opinion on the matter—he did not need to. "It's a fine room, Your Grace, and yours for as long as you choose to stay. Moon guard your sleep."

"And yours, Steward. Good night," Kinnaird rose as a servant appeared and followed him through a doorway that led up a short flight of stairs to the private solar, which normally would have been used by the lord and lady of the keep.

He wondered what was below him, as normally the solar was on the ground floor, behind the great hall, on the protected side of the keep. Well, a mystery for another day. He had enough with which to contend for the moment. Shucking his clothing, Kinnaird quickly climbed into bed. As he settled, he noticed that someone had set out fresh clothes on a trunk near the fireplace that were far more suited to the region.

Out of habit, he settled a heat spell on his bedclothes, should the heat shields actually fail in the night. Sun and moon, he hoped they did not. Next, he checked the heat shields, ensuring that all was indeed well there.

Then he extinguished the candles in the room with a focusing of thought and power and finally burrowed down deeply into the soft, warm blankets, and the surprisingly comfortable bed.

His mind spun with thought after thought, trying to unravel the mystery of it all. Eventually, however, he simply became too tired to stay awake. He drifted off to sleep as his mind turned away from intrigue and war and settled on thoughts of Reyes.

THREE

Reyes stifled an urge to roll his eyes as the Earl of Pleasant quibbled with the king over taxes owed.

The king glanced up as the earl finally paused, catching Reyes's eye. Immediately understanding what was needed, Reyes opened his portfolio and slid out the reports he had been carefully compiling over the past month. He slid the main set toward the king and a copy toward the earl.

"As you can see," the king said, flipping through the reports, "your arguments are futile. Now, if you would like to make up for the time you have wasted, you may explain these numbers to me." His voice was idle on the surface, but heavy with the possibility of serious penalties just beneath.

The earl was silent.

"You are almost two years behind on your taxes," the king continued. "I have done you a courtesy by calling you here to speak privately. I will continue to keep the matter private. Only Reyes and I know anything about it, past the individual in the tax offices who first brought the matter to my attention. You have until the end of the month, my good Earl, to pay at least fifteen percent of what you owe. I expect the rest by the end of the year. This year's taxes are figured into the numbers, so you need only worry about the final sum."

The earl remained silent for a couple more minutes, then finally replied, "Yes, Your Majesty."

"Then I believe this meeting is concluded," the

king said. "Thank you for your time."

"Majesty," the earl repeated stiffly, then rose, bowed, and left the room.

Falling back in his seat and sighing, the king said, "Ring us some coffee, Reyes, would you?"

"Of course," Reyes replied, and tugged the blue bell pull. Coffee requested, he closed the portfolio that had held the reports and opened the one that held the king's schedule for the day. "You are clear for the next hour, then you have a meeting in the garden with Lord Charles at half past dusk bells. I've got you meeting your councilmen for drinks at evening holy bells and supper with the ambassadors at the half mark bells. Is there anything that requires adjusting that has slipped past my notice?"

The king shook his head. "No, I do not think so. You might see that the usual assortment of lords is invited to drinks; it will make them feel special."

"Yes, Majesty." The king gave an amused snort. Reyes smiled and corrected himself, "Yes, Rhoten."

Nodding, satisfied, Rhoten said, "I do not suppose we have heard from any of a certain three parties, and you've simply not had the chance to inform me?"

A knock at the door prevented Reyes from immediately replying, and he chatted with Maggie for a few minutes before she bustled off again. Once she had gone, he poured the coffee and finally replied, "Alas, no. I am sorry. No news from the north or south as of yet. But it has only been two days. No doubt they want to be absolutely certain before they write."

"More than likely," Rhoten replied. "Anyway, I do not doubt Kinnaird will do his very best to be home in time to put fresh flowers upon your desk come the new week."

Reyes rolled his eyes and ignored that

comment, pointedly not looking at the roses still perched on the corner of his desk across the room.

Another knock came at the door, and Reyes stood up to get it rather than telling the knocker to enter. This was Rhoten's only break until he finally went to bed, and Reyes would not surrender it lightly. "Yes?" he asked, and immediately relaxed as he realized it was only a court runner with the afternoon post. "Thank you."

"Sir," the runner said politely, bowing then darting off to deliver the rest of his bundles.

Carrying the bundle tucked under one arm, Reyes strode first to his desk to fetch his letter opener, then returned to the table to open the post while finishing his coffee. He set everything down to refresh their coffees then turned to his lamp, trimming it and turning up the flame. Extended Night was always a difficulty—the mages must work harder, more oil must be used more often, and never was there more than the faintest hint of light teasing at the horizon.

Light adjusted, he picked up his letter opener. It was a handsome piece, like every piece in the magnificent desk set that had been a gift from the Rhoten when he had dismissed everyone else and kept only Reyes. The letter opener was perhaps the finest part of the set, a miniature version of the royal ceremonial sword, accurate right down to the motto carved into the blade and the hilt encrusted with diamonds, amber, and pearls. Rhoten had once joked that the letter opener was probably far sharper than the ceremonial sword had ever been.

He quickly sliced through all the seals on the thirty-odd letters in the pile, sorting them by importance as he went. When he had finished, he set the letter opener aside, flipped his portfolio open to a fresh page, readied a quill, and opened the first letter.

After a few minutes reading he said, "Your daughter is requesting additional funds, Sire."

Rhoten sighed. "Indeed. Where is her guardian's letter?"

"Right here," Reyes replied, and picked up the next letter in the stack, reading through it quickly. Per the king's instructions, Princess Alana's guardian regularly reported to the king what she did and how much she spent, since Alana was all too fond of hiding details from her father. Bedridden since birth due to her weak constitution, she had long ago mastered the art of finding creative ways of keeping herself amused—ways that displeased her father and not infrequently raised several brows at court. "I would not send the funds, Sire." He extended both letters across the table.

Rhoten sighed and took them, reading over them briefly. "You are right. Do not approve further funds being sent to her. Speak personally with the treasury in the morning. I think I shall also compose a letter to her—a very lengthy one."

"As you wish," Reyes replied and flipped to the next day's schedule, making the necessary adjustments to the morning. "Are you certain you would not like something more substantial than coffee before your garden meeting?"

"No, thank you," Rhoten replied. "I will be fine through it and more likely to stay awake while he drones on. But see to it something light is sent to my rooms while I am changing to evening wear?"

Reyes smiled. "Already done."

"Of course," Rhoten said, grinning. "I scarcely believe I ever managed without you. If only the rest of this place was half so efficient and reliable. I think I should make you heir, hmm?"

Reyes choked on his coffee and glared. "Perish the thought, Majesty. Anyway, they would kill me before the reading of the King's Will was complete. I want no part of your job. I am as close to it as I ever want to be."

"Still, the looks upon their faces," Rhoten said, chuckling and shaking his head.

"Indeed," Reyes said dryly. "I live to serve, Majesty, in whatever capacity you desire."

Rhoten sniggered then drained the last of his coffee, smiling in thanks when Reyes immediately refilled it.

Reyes watched a moment as Rhoten turned to stare absently out the window, briefly lost in thought. He smiled faintly, always happy to see Rhoten genuinely happy, if only for a moment. He had never had an easy life. Made king at only twenty-one, parents both dead of sudden illness, sick himself, and the country terrified he would die as well. Only to be rushed into marriage as he was practically still climbing from his sickbed to a woman who was selfish, callous, ungrateful, lazy—and had only managed to produce one sickly daughter with a remarkably similar temperament—before falling off a horse due to an excess of wine. Throughout, there had also been myriad problems at the border, untrustworthy secretaries, and all the usual hazards and difficulties of court life and running a country.

The hard life showed in the deep lines of Rhoten's face, and the shadows of his eyes were far too deep for a man only recently turned forty-eight. His hair, like everyone in the royal family, had once been a fine, bright gold. Time had turned most of it silver, with only the faintest bits of gold still in his hair and close-cropped beard.

Reyes knew Rhoten's life had been happy once, for a very brief period of time. He would give anything to see Rhoten happy again, after all that he had done for

Reyes, all that he continued to do. If these brief snatches were all he could manage, Reyes would continue to manage them and always strive for better.

"I suppose I had best get to the garden," Rhoten said with a sigh. "If I am still there after the three-quarter mark bells, come find me."

"Of course. Sun and moon favor you."

"Thank you, I shall need it."

Then he was gone, and Reyes was alone in his office. Pouring himself more coffee and slicing a piece of the accompanying spice cake, he ate and drank while he resumed going through the post. When he had finished, he told himself his disappointment at a lack of communication from the north was only because he wanted to have done with the matter. It was upsetting Rhoten, and he despised that. He was not disappointed because the palace always seemed different when Kinnaird was absent.

It was certainly quieter when he was gone, even if Kinnaird being in the palace meant he was not out breaking limbs doing foolish things. Reyes made a face and sternly went over all the reasons any sort of relationship was a bad idea. Intimacy was intimacy, and intimacy meant complications. Being the only secretary to the king was all the complication he could manage. He did not want to think of what would become of his life should he add 'Duke's lover' to the pile.

Shaking his head, he finished his coffee and cake, then carried the pile of correspondence to the desk. He locked it away in a drawer to file properly later, then drummed his fingers on the desk as he thought.

He needed to go down to the kitchens to ensure they would deliver Rhoten's meal to his room in two-mark bells, then he needed to go to his own room to change into evening attire before he went to rescue Rhoten from the garden. Better take his portfolio along, because he would not have time to fetch it should he need it later.

Nodding, satisfied with the course plotted, he picked up his portfolio—

And dropped it with a startled cry as his office door banged open and crashed against the wall. "Master O'Bannon! There's trouble in the court. The king requires your presence at once."

Snatching up his portfolio, Reyes bolted from the room and through the myriad hallways of the maze-like palace until he reached the court, the grand receiving room where most people met and milled about and held general audience with the king.

Pushing people out of his way, ignoring their looks and exclamations, he finally reached Rhoten's side. "Majesty?"

"Reyes, this man is an imposter. Take down everything he says and see that it is disproven."

"Yes, Majesty," Reyes replied, and flipped open his portfolio, pulling out a pencil from the case he kept in his jacket. He looked quizzically at the man in question—and felt a sudden, sickening lurch in his stomach. It couldn't be.

But the man had the curly golden hair, the slightly crooked nose, the stature—he looked very much like Rhoten.

"You are, sir?" Reyes asked briskly, setting aside his shock and focusing on what needed to be done.

The man smiled, and something about it irritated Reyes, though he could not say precisely why. "My name is Gandy Aquebor, and thirty years ago my mother had a very brief affair with His Majesty. The king is my father."

"That is a lie," Reyes said flatly. "The king has no sons, and if you were his son, you would not have waited thirty years to come forward. You look like him, I will grant you that, sir, but hair is easy enough to change with dye or magic. I hope you have better proof than that."

Gandy bared his teeth in another irritating smile. "Would I dare to make such a claim if I could not back it up?"

"Yes," Reyes replied, as around him lords and ladies began to murmur or shout their agreement. One of the king's advisors finally stepped forward, and Reyes stepped back to take notes.

"Then state your proof, sir," the advisor said.

"Thirty years ago, when he was only eighteen, the king spent an evening with my mother."

Next to Reyes, Rhoten made a soft, horrified noise of disbelief. Reyes glanced at him and realized with a nasty shock it was true—he had spent the night with some woman thirty years ago. That would have been three years before he took the throne and was married. It made sense.

"So why have you waited so long?"

Gandy laughed. "After she discovered her state, my mother left the country. For years she did not tell me the truth of my parentage. But some things are hard to hide, especially when you hear things about the great King of Elamas."

"Yes, indeed," the advisor said coldly. "If you are the king's son, you will have the royal magic. Prove that to us, and this discussion is obviously over."

"Alas, my lord, Majesty, I cannot. My mother has kept me on suppressants my entire life. For years I thought it was because we lived in a country that is strongly against magic and outlaws it. But when she told me the truth, I realized it was because I could have hurt people otherwise. Alas, I *have* been on them my *entire* life."

Which meant that it would take months for his ability to use any magic to return. That was more than a little convenient.

"He does have magic," said another advisor, eyes vague as he sensed Gandy's magic. "But as he says, it is heavily muted." He shook his head, and his vision sharpened. "I would say it will be a good six months or so before he can prove or disprove his lineage by way of magic. What else can you tell us, sir? You have us curious, and that is not the same thing as content. His Majesty was always faithful to his wife, and out of the country or not, thirty years is a very long time to keep such a secret. We cannot simply accept you as the crown prince, not without much better proof."

"As I said, he met my mother thirty years ago when he was eighteen and she nineteen. It was during a hunting trip to the far south as a guest of the Marquis of Hikks. He met her in the village, in a small tavern called the Frozen River."

Rhoten stirred. "That is very true. I met her there, and we spent the night. But it was not possible for her to have borne a child."

"Because she was barren? Imagine her surprise," Gandy replied. "It was quite the shock, and she left quickly to avoid the humiliation."

Murmurs floated around the court as people promptly forgot all their own indiscretions in favor of judging the king. Reyes could pick out at least four people who had born bastards just with a quick glance around the room. Their country's population was low, and in the more rural areas especially, where magic could not be relied upon as easily as it could in the larger towns and cities, bearing children was difficult.

That being the case, bastards were overlooked more often than they otherwise might have been, and the chance to put a real crown prince on the throne…

Apparently it did not matter that the Princess Alana's betrothed was a very good man and thought well of by the king and court. Duke Keene was by far a better choice than any bastard, but some people would say Gandy was better simply because he was royal blood.

But Reyes did not like Gandy; something about him seemed wrong. That aside, Rhoten was clearly upset, and no good son would simply march into the middle of court and make such an announcement. Such a thing should be handled with discretion and class, not performed like some festival spectacle.

It would, in fact, have been much better if he had said nothing at all. Being king took a great deal more than simply being of royal blood, bastard or no. How dare the man think that just because a young prince had a one-night affair with a tavern wench that he was entitled to the throne.

At least, Reyes thought, he was not pretending to affection or something equally ridiculous. His greedy nature could not have been more apparent.

"My mother had dark hair and blue eyes—I have her eyes, rather than yours, Majesty, which is a shame, I think," Gandy went on. "She often told me she envied your hair, which you wore long back then, and that night had tied back in a blue silk ribbon. You left it behind. She still had it when I buried her last year."

"I see," Rhoten replied, face implacable. He abruptly stood up. "I think that is enough for now. See that he is given a room. I am far from satisfied you are who you claim, but until the matter is firmly settled, you may remain by my good grace. Reyes, come with me."

"Yes, Majesty," Reyes murmured, and followed him from the room. They walked in silence through the halls, ignoring the people they passed, until at last they reached the king's chambers. Reyes's own rooms were a bit further down the hall. A luxury, to have quarters on the King's Hall, but a necessity in his case. Often when the king was woken in the night to tend to emergencies, Reyes's presence was also required.

Rhoten sighed as he walked through the sitting room and into his bedchamber, where he vanished into the dressing room while Reyes took his usual seat at a table by the window. It overlooked the King's Gardens, which Rhoten had ordered crafted into an intricate maze built from stone and ice. Moonlight glistened on it now, adding a sleepy, dreamlike quality.

"Do you think he could be your son?" Reyes finally asked.

"No," Rhoten said. "That woman was barren because she had once miscarried, and it ruined any further chance of her having children. I was hardly the first man she had taken to her bed. The trick will be proving it, and we cannot prove it definitively for at least six months."

Reyes scowled.

"Sun and moon," Rhoten said tiredly, coming out of his dressing room fighting with his neck cloth. "I do not think it will even matter in the end, if my advisors and all the rest decide he would suit well enough."

"The Basden line has always ruled," Reyes said. "They would not accept a pretender, surely. Not over His Grace. You have said yourself he will be a fine king."

"But he is no crown prince, and His Grace cannot overcome that, no matter how good a man and leader he is," Rhoten said. "Girls are favored throughout the kingdom because they can bear children, and there are too many men. Aggravating that, when it comes to the royal family, only a male will suffice." He sighed again. "Send letters, Reyes, and compose them yourself while I go to contend with everyone over the general dinner that will now have to be arranged. Reschedule the drinks and private dinner with the ambassadors. Send them to my daughter, Duke Keene, and Kinnaird. I want them all recalled immediately."

Reyes nodded. "Yes, Majesty."

"Kinnaird especially. He will unravel this disaster better and faster than anyone else. See that Keene's is sent by special messenger and someone you trust to inform him of matters without being a nasty gossip about it. Emphasize that my vote is still with him, and I will not be persuaded by this pretender. His presence would help with that."

"Of course, Majesty," Reyes said, already drafting the letters, mind shifting over his list of messengers and finally settling on one. "Anything in particular I should tell Her Highness?"

"That she had best return home and be a good princess, or there is a good chance she will never be queen," Rhoten replied. "That should set her heels afire."

Reyes smiled briefly, "Yes, Majesty. Sun and moon favor you over dinner."

"Thank you, Reyes. Send round word to me when the letters have been dispatched."

"It shall be done within the hour."

Then Rhoten was gone. Reyes stared after him for a moment then bent to his letters. When he had finished the drafts, he closed his portfolio and returned to his office. Lighting the lamps, he first tugged on the black bell pull twice, summoning two messengers, then went to his desk and sat down to rewrite the letters in pen on good paper. The letters to Keene and Princess Alana he signed with the royal seal, stamping the sealing wax with Rhoten's personal crest.

Someone knocked on the door just as he finished, and he called for them to enter. "Sey," he greeted, nodding to the severe looking black-haired man who stood before him, a frequent messenger of his. "Take this to the Duke of Keene. Explain to him all that transpired this evening, answer as best you are able any questions he may ask. Emphasize to him that he has the king's full support. Do as he bids. Keep this to yourself and speak to no one else of the matter."

"Yes, Master O'Bannon," Sey replied, accepting the letter and tucking it into his jacket.

Reyes returned to his desk and pulled out a small, square slip of paper, scrawling his name on the bottom. "Get what money you require from the treasury, then go." Sey nodded and left.

Reyes turned to the second man, fair of hair and with a heavily freckled face but just as somber as Sey. "Take this letter to Princess Alana," he said, and signed a second slip. "You know how to deal with her, Lorine."

"Yes, Master O'Bannon," Lorine said with a smile. He departed.

Returning to his desk, Reyes composed one last letter and sealed it as he had the others. Then he rose and left the office, making his way quickly to the palace tower where the birds were kept. "I have need of one of your hawks," he told the Master Falconer. "It needs to go to the Northern Treasury."

"Yes, sir," the man replied, and immediately went to fetch a beautiful white and gray bird. Reyes handed him the letter and waited impatiently as the man affixed it to the bird.

Finally, finally it was off, and he watched it until it was well out of sight. He hoped Kinnaird hurried home. As crazy as the man made him, he would fix this mess in a way that no one else could.

46

F⊕UR

A pounding on the door woke him. Kinnaird swore softly as the remnants of a very pleasant dream slipped away. Sitting up in bed, he called for the knocker to enter. A soldier entered, dressed in the special armor worn by those on gate duty who might, at any time, be forced to go out into the dangerous weather. He spilled into the room with frantic urgency and approached the bed with a sealed letter extended, holding his lamp close so Kinnaird could see it.

Kinnaird saw at once that the letter bore the king's seal. That, combined with the guard's urgent manner… No one was sending him good news.

"Sent by royal hawk, Your Grace," the soldier said, lighting a lamp when Kinnaird indicated he should. "We have sent word to the steward, but we brought the letter straight to you."

"Thank you," Kinnaird said, dismissing him. Alone, he briefly examined the sealed letter, looking for anything that might give away a ruse, some other foul play, but all seemed well. The hand which had written his name was definitely Reyes's. He also saw Reyes had written just his name, rather than more properly using his title. That was definitely not like Reyes.

Breaking the seal, he quickly read through the letter. The words made him stare in shock, and despite having reflexively memorized the contents as he read them, Kinnaird read the letter again.

Then he tossed the letter aside and clambered out of bed, headed straight for his clothes. Pulling them on, lacing and buttoning hastily, he yanked on his boots and stamped into them.

Another knock came at the door as he was reaching for his cloak.

"Your Grace," Tamark greeted as he stepped inside. "I was told there was an urgent letter."

Kinnaird nodded. "Yes. I've no time to explain. The letter is there on the bed; no eyes but yours may read it. Destroy it when you are done. I do not know when, or if, I shall return here." He slid a ring from his finger and pressed it into Tamark's hand. "Continue to pursue my inquiries. Come to me at Basden should you learn anything I must know. If you cannot reach me, then insist upon speaking with Reyes O'Bannon. He is the king's secretary."

Tamark nodded and slid the ring onto the middle finger of his left hand, barely glancing at Kinnaird's falcon and sword seal upon it. "Sun and moon grace you and the king."

"And you," Kinnaird replied, then swung his heavy cloak over his shoulders, settling it comfortably. Such things were a pain to transform with, but he could do it. Nodding in farewell, he strode from the room, but rather than head straight out of the keep, he instead strode to and up one of the keep towers.

Reaching the top, he dismissed the guards stationed there, telling them to return in a few minutes time. Alone, he smiled faintly as he climbed atop the crenellation. Growing up, he had watched enviously for years and years as his father did this very thing, making it look so simple and easy. A cousin had once tried it against strict orders and nearly died, and had been too afraid to fly for years.

Eventually, Kinnaird's father had taught him

how to do it while his cousin sat afraid. It could be tricky, changing in such a way, but it was infinitely easier than shifting while grounded. His father had been extremely proud at how quickly Kinnaird had grasped it, had grasped anything to do with their special brand of magic. How quickly he had grasped many things. Kinnaird had always loved their flying lessons best. It was the one place he could be with his father where only a very small handful of people could follow.

He heard someone come up just as he braced himself and half-turned to see Tamark. "Was there something else you needed?"

"Only wanted to see you off, Your Grace," Tamark replied. His mouth quirked, and he continued, "As a friend and out of simple, greedy curiosity."

Kinnaird laughed, appreciating the honesty. "Well, I warn you, it has been known to turn stomachs. Not, I suppose, that you'll see much with the way I am going to do it."

Tamark said nothing, merely returned the smile and nodded.

Turning back toward the landscape, Kinnaird admired briefly the snow, the ice, the jagged edge of mountains and the distant gray of the ocean. Not a conventional sort of beauty, but he would always love this harsh land he called home. Drawing a breath, he threw himself from the tower, breaking the bonds of held back magic as he fell. That was always how it felt—like he was finally letting something free.

His ability to transform was nothing like his more ordinary magic. It was hot as it consumed, painful as he felt things crack and shrink and otherwise alter. Part of the magic was in numbing the full brunt of the pain, but he could still feel some of it.

But it was also one of the most thrilling feelings

when the change took, and he could soar. It was heady, exhilarating. More than even that, it simply felt right, like a pleasant exhaustion after working hard all day. Like falling asleep sated and complete in a lover's arms. Like the rare smiles he coaxed from Reyes that were for him and him alone.

He finished changing before he had fallen even halfway, and his cry made a few guards jump as it broke the quiet of the night. He flew swiftly higher and alighted on the crenellation of the tower, crying out again to Tamark before lifting off into the dark star-strewn sky, circling once before heading back toward Basden. He was anxious to be home, to deal with the would-be usurper.

One way or another.

~~*

He arrived on a well-lit private terrace accessible only by those who lived in this private wing of the castle—himself and half a dozen other people, all high-ranking nobles who shared his rare brand of magic. He transformed as he drew close, landing neatly on his feet and standing smoothly, settling his clothes with practiced ease.

The sound of movement drew him up short, and he stopped in surprise as he saw Reyes step out onto the terrace.

"It's about time," Reyes snapped.

Kinnaird almost smiled, teased, but he had never seen Reyes so visibly worried and strained. Closing the space between them, he reached out wholly without thinking to gently grasp Reyes's chin and tilt his face up for a brief kiss.

He was simultaneously elated and increasingly concerned that Reyes did not, in any way, protest the kiss or even attempt to move away. "I am sorry," Kinnaird replied quietly. "I came immediately after receiving your letter, but storm winds slowed me halfway home. What else has gone wrong since you sent the letters?" He let go of Reyes's chin and slid his hand down to gently grasp Reyes's arm instead, squeezing reassuringly. "You look exhausted, my dear."

Reyes, even more alarmingly, did not protest the endearment. "He will not sleep. He barely eats. He is making himself sick with worry and dread and shame. That stupid twit is not helping matters—quite the opposite."

Kinnaird lifted one brow. 'He' was obviously Rhoten. 'Stupid twit' could only be Princess Alana. The only purpose she served was providing a means by which to put Keene on the throne someday. If Rhoten doted on Reyes like a much-adored second son, then he had definitely molded Keene for the throne as he would have a true eldest son. No better man in the country existed, and Kinnaird would be damned if he let anyone take the throne away. That the foul impostor was also upsetting Reyes to this degree… Yes, he would be rid of the bastard by whatever means necessary.

He kissed Reyes again, wishing briefly he could always steal kisses so easily and casually. "What is the imposter doing now?"

"Making friends and allies, though he's not been here long," Reyes replied, and then seemed to shake himself, drawing slightly away and firmly back into himself.

No more kisses, then, alas.

"People are already saying that perhaps he should be given a chance," Reyes said. "The court is dividing, and I fear the protestors will shrink as the days continue. He has a presence, much as I hate to say it, and charm enough to put even you to shame."

Kinnaird scoffed at this. "Obviously you have not been subjected to my charm for far too long, my dear. Where is he now?" he continued, before Reyes could yell at him for being flippant.

"The garden pavilion," Reyes said. "The Earl of Pleasant is holding a luncheon for him to 'further quiz the king's son and see how he manages amongst the court.; People adore his tales, especially those from the 'land which fears magic.'" His lips curled in distaste.

"The what?" Kinnaird's brows shot up. He only knew one country which detested magic, but they certainly did not *fear* it… "Afraid? Oh, my. He really knows nothing, or cannot tell the difference between fear and contempt. Do me a favor, would you, my dear?"

Reyes looked at him, clearly torn between annoyance and surprise. "What did you need?" he finally asked, and Kinnaird wanted to kiss away the confusion that drew his brows down. He never let Reyes do anything for him, not so much as fix his coffee. He refused ever to let Reyes see him as one more element of duty, to put more formality between them. Reyes had not quite figured his motive out yet.

"My bedchamber," Kinnaird replied. "There is a small box carved from feyestone in the table by my bed. Bring it to me at the garden pavilion."

"As you wish," Reyes said with a nod. He turned away, and Kinnaird could not bear it when the exhaustion and worry slid over his face again.

Tugging Reyes back, Kinnaird kissed him deeply, holding fast and not letting up until Reyes finally began to kiss him back. When finally forced to break the kiss, he said softly against Reyes's mouth, "We will fix it. I promise, I will set all to rights."

Reyes shoved him back, and Kinnaird smiled to

see the more familiar glitter of annoyance in his eyes, but Reyes surprised him when he said, "I know you will. That is why I wrote to you."

Kinnaird could not think what to say against such unexpected faith. He was not at all accustomed to Reyes being nice to him, as badly as he wanted it.

"But," Reyes continued more icily, "that does not grant you leave to kiss me."

Grinning, Kinnaird led the way from the terrace, reluctantly splitting off so that Reyes could continue back through the wing to fetch the box, while Kinnaird turned toward the main part of the palace, through it to the gardens.

Magic being an extremely valuable commodity, it was generally used strictly for essentials and very rarely expended on a large scale for frivolous things. That being so, gardens, as foreigners thought of them, did not exist in Elamas. Instead of thriving greenery and flowers, gardens in Elamas were complicated works of stone and ice and snow. The royal gardens were the result of thousands of hours of slow, careful, laborious work. Statues, benches, footpaths— everything was an intricate display of beauty made from the elements of their hard, unforgiving world. Like the landscape, it was a beauty not everyone could appreciate.

The gardens were especially valued because they were a safe sort of outdoors, unlike the untamed landscapes beyond the palace and cities, where snow and ice could hide far greater dangers.

Certainly the stranger who bore some passing resemblance to the king, sitting next to the Earl of Pleasant in the middle of the pavilion, did not seem to appreciate his surroundings. Perhaps he was simply too busy being admired himself to admire anything or anyone else.

As Kinnaird drew close, several voices and conversations drifted into silence, and all eyes were upon him as he reached the bastard.

The bastard stopped talking as he realized people were no longer paying attention to him. He looked at Kinnaird. "My lord?"

"That would be 'Your Grace,'" Kinnaird replied coldly. "Who, or what, are you?"

"I am Gandy Aquebor, illegitimate son of the king." A pause. "Your Grace."

Kinnaird looked down his nose. "Clearly illegitimate. A legitimate son would have managed to acquire *some* manners."

Around them, people were silent, or whispered and tittered behind gloves and fans.

Gandy finally stood up, something he should have done much sooner, moving with deliberate slowness. "Your Grace, I have heard much about you, even before I managed to make my way here. You are the king's famous falcon, his favorite pet."

Kinnaird gave Gandy a smile that was all teeth. "Only his favorite raptor. I am not really very good at being a proper pet. So tell me, illegitimate son, what did you do before you decided you wanted to try your hand at being Crown Prince?"

Returning the smile, Gandy said, "My mother traveled until she decided to settle in a country far from here. A country that manages to survive without magic, actually. It's quite fascinating how they manage, how much they fear magic."

"I see. But that still does not tell me your profession, your calling. 'Tis no easy thing, being king. What makes you think you are fit for it?"

"I was an entertainer, Your Grace."

"A not unworthy profession. My mother was an actress. But she would not be the first to say that is not a profession which makes you good at being king."

"I want only to know the father I was always denied. It is not my decision whether or not I ever take the throne or even am named a prince. That is for wiser minds than mine to decide."

Oh, he was certainly smooth, Kinnaird would give him that. He could already see many people soaking up the display of humility, the self-deprecating smile.

A stir in the crowd briefly drew his attention, and he half-turned to see Reyes approaching him with Kinnaird's box in his hands.

"Thank you, my dear," Kinnaird said, taking the box and pulling a small ring of keys from an inner pocket of his jacket. Selecting a small one made of silver, he unlocked the box, then tucked the keys away again. Opening the box, he rifled around its wildly varied contents until he at last found what he sought. Then he handed the box back to Reyes and stepped a bit closer to the imposter.

"You said you come from a country that reviles magic. I have been there several times. The entire continent is generally rife with war, between the three countries that cover it. Growing up where you did, I am certain you will appreciate this. Keep it, as a token of welcome." He held out the object he had taken from his box.

Between two small square panes of glass, framed in silver, was a pressed flower. It bore five petals, fat at the base and narrowing to a sharp point. It was the color of fresh blood and had lost none of its color despite the fact it had been trapped in glass for the past three years. Obtaining it had cost Kinnaird a small fortune.

Gandy frowned briefly as he accepted it, but then the expression cleared, and he smiled stiffly.

"Thank you, Your Grace."

"What is it?" Someone asked, and others bustled closer to see it for themselves and await the explanation.

Kinnaird answered before Gandy could form a more theatrical reply. "It is a called a seven-year flower. These flowers take seven years to fully bloom, and they go through several colors before finally reaching red. The country of Salhara, across the western sea and farther west still, knows the secret of turning these flowers into an elixir that gives them the gift of magic. Their neighbor, the country of Kria, hates magic and strives constantly to wipe the seven-year flowers out of existence."

He could see in Gandy's eyes that his message had been received—if Gandy really had been to Kria, he would know all about seven-year flowers and the elixir made from them. It was impossible to live in Kria and not learn about Salhara, their longest and bitterest enemy. If Gandy possessed the seven-year flower elixir that granted magic to those who did not have it, he could no doubt sufficiently fake the special royal magic that he would need to possess if he wanted to make everyone think he was the king's son.

But he had just been informed he would not fool Kinnaird. He knew all the signs of seven-year poisoning; Gandy would not slip by him easily.

"I am astonished Your Grace was able to obtain a red seven-year flower," Gandy finally said.

Kinnaird nodded. "It cost dearly. But please, do take it as a gift. You would appreciate it more than I."

"Then I thank you again, Your Grace. You are too generous by far."

Smiling blandly, Kinnaird nodded again, then turned and strolled away, taking Reyes with him.

"What was that about?" Reyes demanded when

they were well away.

Kinnaird explained quickly, concluding with, "Watch his eyes. Should they change color, or seem to glow, he is drugged and using the elixir or about to use it. Be careful. That magic is nothing like ours. Much more wild and far more dangerous. The Salharans use it for many things, but its primary use for them is martial. They can use it with deadly force, and it's all too possible Gandy has acquired those skills."

"Is Salhara involved in this, do you think?" Reyes asked.

Kinnaird purse his lips as he thought, but he shook his head after a moment, further consideration not changing his initial opinion. "No. Salhara is voraciously protective of its flowers and their secrets. They have never expressed interest in international matters before, and they need nothing we can offer. No, I think Galand is behind the attacks, and it is interesting that a bastard shows up at this time. But I think we are also very far from seeing the entire picture."

Reyes nodded. "Keene arrived while you were in the gardens. He is waiting for you in my office. I am going to check on Rhoten, then I will join you if you require it."

"Of course." Kinnaird smiled. "I think—"

"You have taken enough liberties," Reyes said, cutting him off, voice tart. "Do not try to take more."

"Well, you cannot blame me for trying," Kinnaird replied, winking. "I like kissing you."

Reyes rolled his eyes. "I will see you later, Your Grace."

"Yes, my dear."

He watched Reyes walk away, admiring the fine lines of his body, the tidy, elegant way he moved, the way the torchlight struck his dark hair and warmed his skin. Then he turned his mind back to business and strode to Reyes's office.

Inside, a tall, broad-shouldered, handsome figure stood by the window, the light from the fireplace highlighting his profile. Black hair, sharp green eyes, and the sort of drawing, commanding presence that helped make a good king.

"Dilane," Kinnaird greeted.

Turning from the window, Dilane Lymon, Duke of Keene, smiled tiredly. "Kinnaird. Have you encountered this pretender yet?"

"Encountered and warned. I think he knows a few Salharan tricks to fake his way through the royal magic, but he must not have it quite mastered yet, because Reyes mentioned to me in a letter than he put forth the excuse of blockers to stall people. He resembles the king, but only in passing. I think we can be easily rid of him. If worst comes to worst, I'll use foul means rather than fair to rid us of him."

Dilane shook his head. "Our position will be all the stronger if we can discredit him legitimately. Violence will only make people believe the king is guilty. But I think we will have to keep the option in mind, depending on how this Gandy behaves and what he does."

"I agree," Kinnaird replied. "Reyes says the king is not taking it well."

"He should not have to take it at all," Dilane said. "I wish people would stop heaping further difficulties upon his life. Even for a king, he has endured enough. At that, I suppose I should go visit with Her Highness."

Kinnaird nodded. "Good luck. Reyes mentioned briefly to me that the 'stupid twit' was helping nothing."

Dilane made a face. "I see. How typical. She is in for a rude awakening when she is my wife, I promise you that. I will see what I can do."

"Better you than me, my friend." Kinnaird finally abandoned the doorway and crossed the room. Dilane met him halfway, and they embraced briefly. Then Kinnaird went to the small bar tucked into one corner and poured them both drinks. "So how was your journey home?"

"Uneventful," Dilane replied, swirling the pale gold liquid in his glass. "The quiet was nice. I believe my brother will do quite well with the title and estate when I pass them to him." He grimaced. "Assuming, of course, that I will still be in a position to do precisely that in a few months' time."

Kinnaird squeezed his arm reassuringly. "We will not let that bastard take the throne away, I vow it. No upstart foreign imposter will displace the Fox of Elamas. You were born for the throne, Dilane. You will get it."

Dilane smiled faintly. "This would all be a good deal easier to manage if I really *had* been born to the throne. I would not protest if a better man came along, of course, but..."

"This one is no better than a rat, I promise you."

"Then we must discredit him," Dilane said. "What sort of investigations have been started? If he is a liar, some evidence of that will exist somewhere."

They paused as the door suddenly opened, and Reyes stepped inside. He looked at them both then strode to his desk, accidentally brushing against the roses as he circled around it. Several petals fell to the floor, bright splashes of color against the deeper shades of the rug.

Kinnaird stared at them, realizing that the following day was his day to go down to the city proper and purchase a fresh bouquet of flowers. Hopefully he would have the opportunity. In the years since he had started the tradition, he had only ever failed to deliver when he was away from the palace. Perhaps he could slip away tonight.

Reyes sat down and pulled out the portfolio that seldom left his person. "Now that both of you are here, I can bring you fully up to date. I have sent out men to learn whatever they possibly can about Gandy Aquebor. I also sent a letter to our contacts in Kria, though that will not turn up much, I expect. In the meantime, he continues to ingratiate himself to the court. Already he has the full support of the Earl of Pleasant. The king dares not act against him for fear of making himself look all the more guilty."

"Right," Dilane said. "What of Her Highness?"

"She is furious, 'ashamed' of her father. She has not left her rooms since returning to the palace in a tizzy, though she makes certain her opinions are spread far and wide."

Dilane frowned, clearly angry. "I will deal with Her Highness. In fact, I will go do that now. Thank you, Reyes, for summoning me so quickly. Kinnaird." He nodded in farewell and left.

Leaving Kinnaird alone with Reyes. Refilling his own glass, he then poured one for Reyes and carried it to the desk, setting it down with a soft clink. "Drink."

Reyes opened his mouth, clearly to argue, but then simply shut it again. Picking up the glass, he tossed the contents back in one quick, neat shot. Kinnaird smiled at how smooth and unthinking the gesture had been.

High, noble fashion was all about delicate sips, with lots of swirling and sniffing in between, making a show of appreciating the nuances of the alcohol. The manner in which Reyes drank, that reflexive toss back he had probably barely realized he'd done, was pure lower class.

Kinnaird loved the little hint into Reyes's life before the palace. He had all the manners and movements and… finer points of someone with breeding, but every now and again he hinted at something more, a broader, less rigid life than that of the strictly upper class.

He reached out and picked off a stray rose petal from the shoulder of Reyes's jacket.

Reyes stared at the petal then lifted his gaze to meet Kinnaird's eyes. "You should get some rest. Sun and moon alone know what will happen next."

"You should come rest with me," Kinnaird replied.

"No," Reyes replied with a scathing look. "I wish you would accept my refusal, Your Grace. I am not, and never will be, fit for courting. You should leave me behind and move on."

Kinnaird frowned and asked on sudden impulse. "Is that so? Is it really my station which bothers you so much, despite the king's approval? If I were not a duke, would you regard me differently?"

"You are a duke," Reyes retorted. "The question is pointless. Goodnight, Your Grace."

"Goodnight," Kinnaird said and obediently left.

Reyes must be more shaken by all of this than he wanted to admit to unwittingly reveal so much. He had not exactly answered the question, simply evaded it. Would Reyes take him more seriously if he were not a duke?

Five

Reyes called himself a thousand different kinds of fool as he braided his hair, fussing over it meticulously, tying it off with a dark blue ribbon that exactly matched his jacket, breeches, and silver-accented waistcoat.

"Stupid, stupid, stupid," he muttered, staring at his eyes in the mirror, trying hard not to think about kisses for the thousandth time.

Except he could not forget them, nor the way it had felt to be held by Kinnaird. For a few minutes, it really had felt as if everything would work out, as if all their problems would go away.

But some problems *never* went away, and Kinnaird's kisses could not solve them.

Even if they were really rather magnificent kisses.

Heaving an aggravated sigh at himself, Reyes shoved his spectacles onto his nose and turned sharply from the mirror, finishing up the silver buttons on his jacket. Then he stepped into his silver-buckled, dark blue shoes. Last, he picked up his portfolio, extinguished the lamp, and headed for the door.

Reluctantly giving up the sanctuary of his bedchamber, he strode down the hallway to Rhoten's chambers and slipped inside as one of the guards opened a door for him. He stopped short in surprise to see that everyone else was already seated and eating breakfast and glanced at the clock across the room. No, he was five minutes early.

Stung that the meeting time had changed and no one had told him, Reyes crossed silently to the table and took his seat to the king's left, greeting Rhoten with a subdued, "Good morning."

"Good morning, Reyes," Rhoten greeted cheerfully. "I would have called for you, since everyone showed up early for lack of being able to sleep, but you *were* asleep, and I was loath to wake you."

"Thank you, Majesty," Reyes murmured in reply, feeling a little better, even if it was foolish they had not woken him. Motioning the servant away, he poured his own coffee and glanced around the table. Everyone did, indeed, look tired. Especially the twins, who had arrived only a few hours ago, according to the missive he had read upon waking. Rhoten looked as strained as ever, and exhaustion did not help that one bit.

His gaze fell last on Kinnaird, who somehow managed to look up at precisely that moment and catch his gaze. He smiled, slow and warm and somehow intimate.

Reyes flushed and jerked his gaze away, struggling to remind himself how reckless and stupid it would be to give in. He simply could not risk it.

"So what word do you bring from the priests?" the king asked.

Breit set his coffee down and replied, "Shortly after our arrival we found a priest dead, ostensibly of accidently dropping his private shields while out in the field and dying of the cold. We suspect the death was not accidental, but do not know if it was murder or suicide. Regardless, he was the one who leaked inside information to the robbers."

"That is a pity," Rhoten said. "But the

monastery is secure? That is a strategic advantage, should anyone care to take it. They tend not to, the river points being far preferable, but it has been tried before."

"I set all the extra guards I could spare," Erices said. "Hopefully a repeat attack is not forthcoming. What did you learn at the treasury, Kinnaird?"

Kinnaird took a swallow of his coffee then replied, "Lord Morland, the man in charge of the place, is a fool too busy drinking and rutting to do his job. He needs to be stripped of his title. Give it to Steward Tamark."

Rhoten nodded. "Reyes, see that the proper paperwork is begun."

"Yes, Majesty," Reyes replied and flipped open his portfolio.

"The attack was well coordinated and required extensive insider knowledge," Kinnaird continued. "I was recalled before I could complete my investigation. Tamark is finishing my work. I expect his report in not more than a few days."

Reyes made notes of all that was being said and then penned a quick letter to the Master Scribe who was in charge of drawing up the official papers needed to oust one baron and put another in his place. Folding it, he signaled a servant forward. "Deliver this to the Master Scribe at once. No reply is necessary."

"Yes, sir," the servant replied. "The runner has arrived and would like to know if you want the post here or delivered to your office."

"Here," Reyes said.

"Sir," the servant said and bowed himself out. He returned a couple of minutes later with a bundle of post.

Thanking him, Reyes went to the king's small writing desk and borrowed his letter opener. Resuming his seat, he quickly slit all the letters open, stacking them in order of relative importance as he went. Finished, he set the opener aside and began to read.

He swore softly when he reached the fourth one and looked up—and realized everyone had stopped talking and was staring at him.

"What's wrong?" Rhoten asked.

"A ship was attacked only an hour or so after leaving Zale. Two pirate ships came upon it, and it was only sheer chance that a navy ship happened to be close by, working on something else entirely. The pirates were routed, save those captured, and of course they were immediately killed."

Pirates were treated with no mercy. No trials, no imprisonment, just immediate execution. They were the scourge of the trading world. To date, no one had ever been able to bring the pirate nation of Welestra to heel.

"Commissioned, likely," Dilane said. His lands were along the coast, and he was all too bitterly familiar with pirates. "They would never attack so close to land, not for their own purposes."

Reyes handed the letter over for them to further examine and went back to work. The day to day matters of the nation did not stop because of a crisis, and more was the pity.

He swore again and immediately the table stopped. "What now?" Kinnaird asked, looking concerned and amused.

"Talon was attacked last night," Reyes said. "The bridge was set on fire. Why in the name of sun and moon is no one marking these damned letters urgent? Why are they not sending runners to deliver it in person?"

"Because they're not urgent," Kinnaird said, taking the letter and quickly reading it. "If we assume they are all connected, then this is four attacks that were all successfully stopped. They all have extreme potential to be bad—the treasury, the monastery, Zale is our second largest coastal city, and Talon one of the larger river cities. Any one of those could have fallen with dire consequences. But they did not; we stopped them. So in the end, only basic reports were sent out rather than the cries for help that would have otherwise been sent. All that is left for us to do is to follow up, investigate whatever meager clues remain." He worried his bottom lip in thought, making it wet and swollen.

Reyes yanked his gaze hastily away.

"To what purpose, though?" Erices asked.

Kinnaird shook his head. "I do not know. Not yet." He raked a hand through his hair. "I had best go investigate, see if I can find the pieces we need and put them together."

An immediate protest rose up in Reyes's throat, and he drank his coffee to drown it. What was wrong with him? Kinnaird was always coming and going. It was anyone's guess where he was at any given time once he left the palace. He had only remained at the palace for as long as he had, until a few days ago, because of an extremely nasty break to his right leg. Now he was fully healed, he would be like the wind again.

Yet another reason that any relationship would be a mistake.

Still, the knowledge that Kinnaird was already leaving again, likely to be gone for days, tied Reyes back up into all the knots that had finally unwound when Kinnaird had landed on the terrace and kissed him senseless.

The coffee settled poorly on his stomach, and Reyes set it down on the table. He did not even bother to attempt eating breakfast. Instead, he put his attention back on the post, sick with dread at what letter he would find next detailing some disaster. When he got through the stack without further incident, he barely stifled a sigh of relief.

"So I will leave this afternoon," Kinnaird was saying as Reyes rejoined the conversation. "I will start with Zale, and then travel to Talon. Reyes, if you would write letters to them stating we received word, and imply we have no intention of pursuing an investigation? I would like to catch them off guard, if I can."

Reyes nodded, trying not to be stupidly happy that Kinnaird was actually asking him to do something—and something more important than simply fetching a box. "I will send them within the hour. They should get there before midday, easily, if I send them by wing."

"Excellent. Keep me apprised of the situation with the interloper."

"Of course," Reyes replied.

"Then I am off to—" Kinnaird's words were drowned out by a sudden, frantic knocking.

The knocker did not wait for a reply, but spilled into the room and dropped, gasping for breath and red-faced with exertion, at the feet of the king. "Majesty. Cassala was attacked just a few hours ago. Control of the heat shields was taken and used against us. They set the city and bridge aflame."

"My people?" Rhoten demanded.

"There were thousands killed, by earliest estimations, Majesty, from either flame or cold."

Rhoten made a rough sound and stood up. "Kinnaird, Dilane. Go at once. Dilane, take this. I do not care who is walking around pretending to be my son, this is yours. Use it to fix Cassala and find out what is happening!" He yanked a ring from his finger—the one that would normally be worn by the crown prince—and tossed it to Dilane.

Dilane caught it neatly and looked at in surprise. Then he simply nodded and slid it onto the ring finger of his right hand. "Yes, Majesty. Kinnaird, pack whatever you need and bring it to me. My servants can carry it with my belongings while we go on ahead. Meet me at the private terrace. We will leave from there. Try not to leave me too far behind, would you?"

Erices stood up. "We should—"

"Protect the king," Dilane said, cutting him off. "I cannot believe that a bastard prince would show up as all these attacks begin to occur. I want you and Breit to stay close—especially Breit, whom they will not anticipate being capable of protecting anyone."

Breit nodded and turned briefly to look up at his brother. They stared at each other a moment in silence, then Erices sat back down, looking disgruntled but resigned.

"Reyes," Rhoten said. "Draw up the appropriate letters and warrants Kinnaird and Dilane will need to act as my voice while in Cassala in case anyone decides the ring is not enough. I want to know who just slaughtered thousands of my people."

"Yes, Majesty," Reyes replied and stood up. Gathering his things, carefully not looking at Kinnaird, he left.

He fled to his office then stopped, torn between frustration, amusement, vexation, worry, and a deep, warm fondness that scared and depressed him.

Perched on the corner of his desk, in a green crystal vase, was a bouquet of tiger lilies.

They were rare—extremely rare, like any genuine flower in so cold a climate. But the tiger lilies were especially rare. They were his favorite, though, and Kinnaird knew that. Kinnaird had been the one to tell him what the flower was the first time Reyes had seen it.

He had only been at the palace a couple of weeks then, young and overwhelmed, just one more secretary in the general pool. Back then the palace really had been a maze to him, and he had gotten completely lost. At one point, he had wound up in a banquet hall only recently prepared for some lavish dinner. Each table had been decorated with the most beautiful orange flowers, like nothing he had ever seen.

It had been Kinnaird who had come across him and chatted with him, explained the flowers, before finally guiding him back to more familiar sections of the castle. That had been the first time he had properly met and spoken with the notorious Duke of Keyes, though it had hardly been the first time he had seen Kinnaird.

Reyes wondered if that day had been when his infatuation had begun or simply when he had acknowledged it. He wished he could pinpoint when it had gotten a lot deeper and more complicated than mere infatuation.

Sighing softly, trying not to worry about the all-too-real chance Kinnaird may not return to give him more flowers, he pulled out a single tiger lily and twirled the stem in his fingers. He did not realize he had company until arms wrapped around him from behind, and warm, coffee-and-cream flavored breath washed over his cheek. "Why are you frowning so, my dear?"

Reyes scowled at the flower he held. "Should I be smiling? Let me go."

Ignoring the command, chuckling softly, Kinnaird said, "The flowers are meant to make you smile, yes. Especially the tiger lilies. You were smiling so sweetly that day."

"You remember," Reyes said quietly.

Kinnaird made a soft noise and turned him

around. "How could I forget? I had admired you before, but I think that was the day I decided you would be mine someday."

Reyes said nothing.

"Well, I will convince you eventually. I would press it now, but I've not the time, alas."

"You'll never have the time," Reyes blurted out, then immediately regretted it, wishing he could take the words back.

"What?" Kinnaird looked at him in surprise.

Since he could not take them back, and Kinnaird would not stop harassing him, Reyes went on. "You are the king's falcon. A duke with a lineage as old as the country itself. You fly so high, in so many ways, in so many directions…" He bit his lip and turned away, feeling guilty. He had no right to be jealous of Kinnaird's duties and obligations.

That aside, he had no right reprimanding anyone about making a choice that bound his feet to the chosen path, with no hopes of freeing himself from it.

"I'm sorry," he finally said. "It is not my place to say such things."

"No," Kinnaird replied, mouth curving in a soft smile. "If you have problems, they can be addressed and worked out. Better to have problems than nothing at all. I cannot fight nothing, but I can deal with problems. I wondered before why you avoided the question of my being or not being a duke."

"You are a duke, and it is stupid to waste time asking hypothetical questions."

"My father almost gave up his title to be with my mother," Kinnaird replied with a shrug. "I—"

"No!" Reyes bellowed, startling them both. "That's—that's selfish. A lot of people would suffer if you gave up your title and for what? Nothing worth causing such pain and suffering."

"Reyes…" Kinnaird let go of the grip he still had on Reyes to reach up and cup his face, tugging him in gently for a long, slow kiss.

Stupid… so stupid to give in, but he really did love Kinnaird's kisses, the way everything else faded away for a time, even his worries, the way he felt warm and safe and—and loved, though he should not feel that way. He had no right to presume the feelings ran that deep on both sides.

He was a fool to let them run that deep on one side.

But he could only moan softly and reach up to cover the hands that still gently cupped his face. He barely noticed when Kinnaird tangled their fingers together, then drew their arms down so that their hands rested at the small of Reyes's back.

Until they finally broke apart, and he realized he was neatly pinned in place.

"We will have to continue this conversation upon my return," Kinnaird said with a sigh. "Possibly it will have to wait until all current problems are resolved. But at least promise me we *will* continue it."

Reyes tried to refuse, to tell him no, this was the end of it, goodbye. But if he had ever been capable of resisting Kinnaird, he would not be in this situation to begin with, and so he could only concede defeat and say, "All right. We'll talk."

Kinnaird smiled in that way that always warmed Reyes deeper than any fire shield would ever manage. "Thank you." He playfully kissed Reyes's nose, then took a real kiss, deep and long, leaving Reyes with a deep ache when he finally broke it and let Reyes go.

"Just—" he coughed, suddenly feeling cold now that he was no longer being held. "Just come back alive, you fool. Don't break anymore bones, either."

"I will be careful. Stay safe while I am away. So long as he is here, I sense this place is not truly safe."

Reyes nodded. "I will make certain we are safe. Erices will not let anything happen to us, at the very least."

Kinnaird made a face. "I would feel better if you had any sort of magical skill beyond the very basic you possess. Or even some sort of weapons training. Anyone who attempts to harm the king will not hesitate to get you out of the way first, my dear."

Reyes shrugged. "Sorry. All I can do is write up—" He swore. "You made me forget I was supposed to be drawing up your papers!" He smacked Kinnaird hard in the chest, then moved around his desk and began yanking out all the things he would need to draw up papers that even the Master Scribe was not allowed to do.

Laughing, Kinnaird said, "It is entirely your fault. I came to fetch those papers, and you looked too distressed for me to do anything but try and comfort."

"Be quiet," Reyes said, dipping a quill and writing as quickly as he could without sacrificing neatness.

Kinnaird subsided with a last chuckle.

Reyes worked swiftly, setting the papers to dry while he prepared the special inks for the notarizations and seals. Several minutes later, everything was finally ready, and he handed Kinnaird a leather portfolio with the papers inside. "Two complete sets permitting you to act with the full weight of the throne." He fell silent a moment, then said to Kinnaird's chest, "Come back. *Alive.*"

Kinnaird put a finger beneath his chin and tilted his face up. "I promise."

"Good," Reyes muttered.

"Do I get a kiss goodbye?" Kinnaird teased.

Reyes rolled his eyes, but for once gave in to the impulse he had always fought to sink his hand into Kinnaird's thick hair and drag him down for a very long and through kiss.

They were both out of breath when they finally drew apart.

"I had better go," Kinnaird said, though he clearly wanted to do no such thing. "Send your thoughts, my dear, should I need them to find my way."

"Get," Reyes said, and shoved him toward the door.

Smiling, Kinnaird finally departed.

Reyes moved back to his desk and collapsed in his chair, burying his face in one hand.

He nearly jumped out his chair when the door the king's office opened from the other side, and Rhoten stepped out. No one could get to that office, not even the king, without first going through Reyes's office. "Majesty—Rhoten—How?"

Rhoten burst out laughing. "It is a good thing that everyone else knocks, Reyes. The two of you were so intent upon each other you did not see or hear me walking through. Quite unusual for Kinnaird. You must have him well and truly snared, hmm?" He winked. "Let me know when the first appointment has arrived. Those are beautiful flowers." Then he went back into his office, closing the door quietly behind him.

Reyes sat back down and let his head fall to thump against the top of his desk, groaning in mortification. Royal secretary, and the king had caught him exchanging heavy kisses with the Duke of Keyes. In the *office.*

It really did not soothe him that Rhoten sanctioned their relationship—not that they had one, because they did not, because that would be the epitome of foolish. He was going to kill Kinnaird.

Making a face, Reyes opened his portfolio to check over the day's schedule, made a few adjustments, and set it aside. Pulling out paper and ink and sealing supplies, he began to compose necessary letters, orders, warrants, and other such things, ringing constantly for servants and runners, keeping himself too busy to think.

SIX

Kinnaird stood impassively as more bodies were carried away from the smoking wreckage that was a good portion of the Great Bridge of Cassala. The gruesome work was made all the worse by the fact that it must be done during Extended Night; the absolute dark required additional lighting, further straining and taxing people who already had grief and fear burdening them.

There were six major cities of trade in Elamas. Two of them were strictly on the coast. Three of them were strictly on the river. One, the greatest of them, Cassala, was built where river met ocean.

The Great Bridge was nearly as old as the country itself. One of his ancestors had helped in its building. He had a distant cousin who captained one of the great trade ships of Elamas and had himself a number of shares in the greater merchant houses.

As no doubt intended, the tragedy went far beyond the lives lost. Homes were lost, businesses, livelihoods… It hurt, period. Nothing else could dishearten and discourage a people faster. Kinnaird wondered if perhaps that was the point. If so, why bother with all the failed attacks? Why go to so much trouble to engineer failure and then this terrible success?

"The whole thing does rather make one wonder what they could have done at the other locations," Dilane murmured beside him. "Whoever is doing this,

I greatly fear those failures could all too easily have been successes."

"Yes," Kinnaird replied. "I fear that is the message they are trying to send, though the ultimate purpose eludes me. The question then becomes, who has the ability to obtain the information necessary to orchestrate so onerous an undertaking as these various attacks? Never mind nearly destroy Cassala."

Dilane's mouth tightened, eyes dark with emotion as he surveyed the terrible chaos slowly being set to rights below. "Someone powerful. Someone who should not have abused their power so." His voice dropped even lower, thin and miserable. "We are supposed to be stronger than this, Kinnaird."

"We are," Kinnaird agreed and smiled at him. "Go be Crown Prince. Do not let your people despair. Leave the finding of the traitor to me. That is my purpose."

Nodding, Dilane clasped his shoulder then slowly withdrew to go to the people hovering a short distance away, plainly waiting none too patiently for him. "As you say, Falcon. Find the traitor. Be careful. I do not want to be the one to tell your poor little secretary you are dead or grievously wounded."

Kinnaird grinned. "If you like us *both* breathing, do not let him hear you call him my poor little secretary."

Dilane briefly returned the smile, then headed off, leaving Kinnaird to watch the cleanup alone. He let his mind drift.

The Northern Treasury.

The Southern Monastery.

A great ship of the trade fleets.

The river city of Talon.

Cassala.

Such a wide range of locations. They were days

and even weeks apart from one another. Yet the attacks were all close together, sometimes only hours apart. That took people, money, and extensive effort. It took knowledge. It also took time. The attack on Cassala alone would have taken months, even years, to plan.

What did the attacks have to do with Gandy? There was too much coincidence in his arrival for him not to be part of it, but to what purpose? It would make sense if the attacks were used in such a way as to discredit rhoten and puff up Gandy by setting him up to solve the sudden flood of problems. But he was doing no such thing, not even trying.

It gave Kinnaird a headache, trying to create the pieces he could not locate.

"Your Grace?" a voice asked, the tone cautious, hesitant.

"Yes?" Kinnaird asked, turning around to see a man of some thirty, forty years standing smartly at attention. He wore sturdy, heavy-weight brown pants tucked into durable work boots. His jacket was a mellow red-brown with the symbol of a sun sinking into the horizon stitched over his heart. The uniform and crest of the Bridge Guild. Opposite the sun crest were the stripes of a Deputy.

"I am Deputy Larsen, Your Grace." He faltered then, briefly, but after a moment regained control of himself. "Well, I am acting Chief, as Chief—he died in the bridge fire. They said you wanted a full accounting, Your Grace. I am here to give it, as best I am able."

Kinnaird nodded and motioned Larsen forward. "I thank you, Deputy, for coming so promptly. I know how busy you must be and how much you must be going through. You have my condolences, for what they are worth."

"Thank you," Larsen said quietly, his eyes going to the wreckage below as he joined Kinnaird on the guard post overlooking the bridge and market grounds. "It was terrible when they ripped the magic from us. They didn't completely succeed, only wrenched the magic from about a third of us, but that was enough, wasn't it? Like having your skin ripped off, only deeper and far more painful. You know?"

"Yes," Kinnaird said quietly. "I know all too well how it feels to have your magic torn away, wrenched from your control."

"So our heat shields went down immediately, and they used the power to start the fires. We were struggling to make the most of what remained to fight off the cold and trying to get our magic back when the bridge…" His face twisted as he looked at the smoldering remains of the major portion of the bridge. It would take years to repair the damage, assuming they didn't have to demolish what was left and start from the beginning. The ice could be traveled, of course, for most of the year, but it was much safer and faster to use the Great Bridge as it was protected by magic and guarded heavily on both ends.

Until the repairs were done, Cassara and Elamas would suffer greatly for its loss. "When does the repair work begin?" Kinnaird asked, because somewhere amidst the tragedy and chaos, the Guild would already be doing what needed to be done.

"In a few more weeks, ideally," Larsen replied. "It is a matter of funds, but the city is already arranging them as best it can. Many will help out of personal pocket, we hope, but they will also be helping the injured and to rebuild the fallen buildings and houses. The bridge… well, it cost enough to build it the first time, didn't it?"

"If you need letters or permits to command special funds, let me know. I will have them drawn up at once." Chances were Reyes had included them in the portfolio already. Reyes was nothing if not thorough.

"Yes, Your Grace. Thank you."

Kinnaird nodded then said, "What I most need from you, Deputy, is anything suspicious you may have seen over the past few weeks or months. I know the chances are slight, but…"

Larsen's mouth twisted. "On the contrary, Your Grace. I have men who were much closer and more involved in the tragedy whom I could have sent to give an accounting. I came myself because I had more to tell you than they could offer, ultimately. To my eternal shame, I suspect I should have said something sooner."

"Speak now."

"I thought the Chief was having an affair," Larsen said, looking out over the city. "That is why I never said anything, why it never struck me as particularly odd, until now. She came every couple of weeks, covered head to toe in that massive cloak, smelling sticky-sweet."

Kinnaird's interest sharpened. "A woman?"

"I always thought so, but as I said, she wore that enormous cloak—a man's cloak. Could have been anyone, even with that scent. It's the scent I remember best, because it was strange for a place like the Bridge Guild building. Didn't strike me as the sort of perfume worn by ladies of the evening, either. Too nice for the cheap ones, too tacky for the expensive ones, eh?"

"Yes," Kinnaird agreed. "I take your point. What was the scent?"

"She smelled like children's sweets. Cherries, definitely. Sugary, but I could not tell you the specifics. I've no nose for it. I only know the cherries because my wife is fond of them, and we buy them once a year for Extended Day."

Kinnaird nodded. "What else?"

"She came every couple of weeks, like I said.

He had a lot of visitors, always socializing, bribing, buttering up, that sort of thing. Politicians." He shrugged. "But that one… She came regular like, more often than the other few regulars. Always thought they had something going on, and he didn't want the wife to know, but as time passed… Well, he wanted her, definitely. He was also afraid of her."

"I see," Kinnaird said. "Know anything else at all about her?"

Larsen grimaced. "No. I learned early on to stay well away from the Chief's guests. One broke my nose when I got too curious back when I was just a bridge spider. Kept my nose clean after that."

"No doubt a wise decision," Kinnaird replied. "Thank you, Deputy. I may come find you later, should I have further questions."

"Of course, Your Grace. If I'm not here, I'll be at our main office." He bowed, then turned and left.

Kinnaird turned over the new bits of information in his mind, pondering. But with so little to go on, he had no hope of deducing the woman's identity. Someone from Galand, no doubt. In such a vast trade city, no one would notice one foreign merchant out of the thousands that flooded the city every day.

Sticky sweet. He felt he should know that scent but was not certain why. Honestly, it could belong to anyone—male or female. The Deputy had said he *thought* the person female but could not say with absolute certainty.

Well, he could not investigate the stranger. That would in all likelihood get him nowhere. So he would begin with the chief and hope that he learned something of the stranger by happenstance. He abandoned his lookout post and made his way back down to the city proper, blending into the crowds of people too restless, too anxious, to stay inside as they might otherwise have done.

Navigating through them was no easy task, made all the more difficult by the smoke from lamps, the dim light where people could not afford or did not bother with anything past the mage lamps. He spoke with several people, working through shop keeps and merchants, sailors and dock workers. None really helped much, though he was beginning to get a solid image of the late chief.

A bridge worker—one of those who did the actual hands-on work that they called bridge spiders—looked up as he passed and greeted, "Your Grace. Did you need something?"

Kinnaird smiled self-deprecatingly and spread his hands in a helpless gesture. "I feel that it is I who should be asking you that question. Deputy Larsen looked quite exhausted. It cannot be easy, on top of so much destruction and grief, to have your chief counted amongst the casualties."

The man looked at him for a long minute or two, then grunted and looked back down at his work. "As to that, sun and moon forgive ill words of the dead, the chief did his part well enough, but all that political and social hobnobbing don't repair the bridge, do it? Just slows up the work while we do his favors to soothe the fat cats in the city. Tragedy, aye. But to be honest, Deputy Larsen were already more chief than the chief. He weren't a bad man, exactly—just weren't a good chief. Catch me?"

"Yes, and I appreciate your honesty," Kinnaird replied. No one else had been half so helpful the entire day, other than Deputy Larsen. Kinnaird flipped the man a coin, then moved on, lost in thought.

So the chief mucked about in politics and the like. There was a tricky bridge to cross, indeed, especially in Cassala, where the imports must be so closely watched and feathers constantly soothed against being ruffled. There was the Great Bridge to watch, the ocean harbors, and the countless smugglers who had strong opinions about the hefty tariffs levied against imported goods.

Who better to have in one's pocket than the Chief of the Bridge Guild? He was in a position to do a great many things should he be so inclined. Kinnaird wondered, angry and sad, what a sticky-sweet scent and a smooth, sticky-sweet touch had persuaded the chief to do.

Hmmm. Men with sticky fingers nearly always had one problem in common—that their fingers were not sticky enough to hold on to their gold. Veering away from the crowds working to do what they could for the bridge, striding past the medical tents where he left gold in the hands of a worn-out looking Master Healer, he made his way to the seedier sections of the city.

There, he wended his way through dark, confusing streets to the gaming hells. If this was not where the chief's sticky fingers mired him, then he had at least been smart enough not to give in to weakness in Cassala. There were several gaming hells of varying sizes, but they were all secretly controlled by one person—the very person who more or less owned the underworld of Cassala, minus the smugglers who were an entity unto themselves.

He entered the largest dend most popular of the hells, ignoring the doormen and the guards posted in the entryway. One of them, obviously new, tried to take issue, but Kinnaird left it to the other guard to inform him as to Kinnaird's identity. He waited in the lobby for the manager to come, and when the man arrived said only, "I wish to speak with him. Now."

Bowing, the manager turned sharply on his heel and led Kinnaird through the back halls, up a set of stairs, down the hall past all the private game rooms, and finally to a set of ornately carved double doors. "Your Grace."

Thanking him, Kinnaird waited until the man had vanished, then let himself inside, closing the doors quietly behind him. Across the room, standing in front of the fire in such a way as to put herself in the best possible light, was a tall, full-figured woman. She was dressed as fine as, if not finer than, any queen, and was easily the most beautiful woman in the country. Precious few knew that the underworld of Cassala was run by a woman.

She presented her hand as he drew close, and he took it in both of his, kissing the knuckles, turning it to kiss the wrist, then finally reaching up to kiss her cheek. "Sharla, it is good to see you." Very good to see her. He had not realized until he saw her that she could easily have been amongst the dead. Thank sun and moon that was not the case.

"Oh, bah," Sharla replied, but smiled, painted blood-red lips glistening in the firelight. They matched perfectly the stiff satin of her bodice. The same lace formed ruffles along the bottom of her red silk skirt. Roses of the exact same shade of red, for she never achieved less than perfection, were pinned into the carefully artless tumble of her honey-gold curls. She was an image entrancing enough to make men drop to their knees, but she had never affected him. It was no small part of the reason she respected and liked him.

He breathed in her scent before drawing completely back. "Roses and musk. Very becoming. I guess you cannot be my mysterious woman with a sticky-sweet scent."

Sharla wrinkled her nose. "If that is what you

favor, my darling Duke, I can point the way to the appropriate houses. Here, we do try to at least pretend to class."

"My dear," Kinnaird drawled, "you could teach class to many of my so-called peers. But you know my tastes, and I am not here to discuss them, anyway."

Nodding, Sharla moved to sit behind her enormous desk. She pulled out a thin cigarette and placed it in a black holder, then lit it at the candle on her desk. Blowing out a thin stream of smoke, she settled back in her seat and said, "About whom do you wish to inquire?"

"The late Bridge Chief."

"Ah," Sharla replied.

Kinnaird could see she was surprised, though her face gave nothing away. He said nothing, but wondered precisely whom she had expected him to ask after.

She blew out another stream of pungent smoke. "He is not one for wasting his money at the tables downstairs. He gambles in social fashion only and never more than he must to keep up appearances. But," she added when Kinnaird started to speak, "he watches it for very good reason. He needs his money to afford the girls he prefers. None of mine, but I do keep an eye on that house."

"I knew it must be funds or flesh."

"Lust is far more dangerous than money," Sharla replied. She reached into her bodice and pulled out a small key which she then used to unlock a desk drawer. Restoring the key to the depths of her ample bosom, she opened the drawer and extracted a small, half-size portfolio. "He owed quite a bit of money when he died, but he always paid his debts in full at the end of each month. A longtime customer, which is why he was permitted to pay in such fashion."

Kinnaird looked the information over, wishing what he read was still capable of shocking him. Nothing about his job shocked him anymore. His mind flitted briefly to Reyes's outburst about Kinnaird never being around. Because it *did* shock him that he thought he might be able to give it all up if it meant staying home with Reyes at his side.

He forced his mind back to work. "So he likes pretty young women to boss him around and punish him." No wonder his mystery woman wore a scent reminiscent of children's candy. It would lend the impression of a younger woman, make him falling-over-eager to obey, to please.

Kinnaird could understand the bossy bit, at least. He loved when Reyes got tetchy and bossy. It made him want to shove Reyes into the nearest wall and jerk him off until Reyes's orders turned into breathless begging.

"Yes," Sharla said. "He was good to the girls, though. He did like women, not children, unlike some in this town I could name but won't this time around. In the end, he wasn't a bad man, really. He just… was not good at his job, and greatly enjoyed when pretty young women took control." She shrugged. "I hope that helps some, dearest."

"It does," Kinnaird replied. The chief had mostly been a good man, but one who liked to try moving in higher society and who was not comfortable with all the control in his hands. That was really all the answer he needed. "Now, darling mine, his was not the name you thought I would say. Who did you think had brought me here this time?"

She smirked. "That will cost you, sweet. As will the chief."

Kinnaird flicked his fingers dismissively. "I can afford you, dove."

"No man can afford me," she replied with a smile that was more cat than bird. She reached into the desk drawer again and selected a second small portfolio, handing it over the desk to him.

Opening it, Kinnaird read for a few minutes then shook his head. "That is a lot of debt our dear Earl of Pleasant is facing. I do not think my estates are worth this much."

"Your estates are worth four times that," Sharla said, rolling her eyes. "As to our dear earl, he has been banned from gambling in Cassala until his debts are paid in full. He is lucky no one dares kill an earl over a matter of money, even a lot of money." She studied her painted nails with a show of boredom. "Rumor has it that he is heavily behind on his taxes, as well, and that the crown is displeased."

"Entirely possible, but taxes are not the sort of problem I handle, so I know nothing about it." If anyone knew those details, it was Reyes, but that was not Sharla's business—and she obviously did not need Reyes to figure such things out. "Speaking of payment, what is your price, fair lady?"

Sharla did not reply immediately, only stared at her cigarette for several minutes. Then she set it aside in a crystal dish and slowly lifted her pale brown eyes to meet Kinnaird's. "I am wasting away here. I am tired of hells and whores. I feel I accomplish nothing with all the skills I have gained, and I am sick of making my living through the criminal activities and vices of others. More than that, I am tired of hiding myself away. I would like to step out of the dark and do something that feels… more worthwhile. I want out of this life. Give me that."

Kinnaird smiled. "It is only an accident of birth, milady, that you were not born a queen. I will see what I can do, though I think such a thing would put you solidly in my debt for some time to come."

She returned the smile. "I know, but if you actually manage it, darling, that is a debt with which I will happily live."

"Then I will see what I can do. It will take time."

Sharla shrugged. "Time I have, though I do not like to be patient." She stood up and moved around the desk, extending her hands and kissing his cheeks as he took her hands in his own. "Let me know if I can be of further assistance to you, Kinnaird."

"I will come calling, never doubt it," Kinnaird replied and kissed her cheek then the backs of her hands.

"Your room should be ready by now, unless you made other arrangements?"

"Why would I make other arrangements when no better can be found? Goodnight, Sharla, and thank you."

"My pleasure," Sharla said. "Sun and moon guard your dreams, especially now that Extended Night is upon us and the city lies so damaged."

"The same to you."

Taking his leave, Kinnaird went back down the hall, then up a set of stairs easy to miss if one did not know to look for them. His room was at the end of the hall. He could go out, continue his investigation, but this late his work would mostly be a waste of time—and he wanted people to cooperate with him. If he kept pushing so much in one day he was more likely to drive them away.

He stripped off his clothes and extinguished the lights, then crawled into bed and lay staring up at the ceiling. His mind flitted from thought to thought, but invariably they settled on Reyes.

Did it really bother Reyes so much, his obligations to the king? If their places were reversed, though, he would not take it well at all if Reyes stumbled into the palace with a badly broken leg, soaked in his own blood.

He was sick with worry as it was, leaving Reyes relatively unguarded with that impostor running about the palace. Really, Reyes should have more care. Anyone who wanted to manipulate the king would know that Rhoten doted upon Reyes. They would not hesitate to hurt or even kill Reyes in order to force Rhoten's hand.

It made his stomach knot with worry. Did Reyes feel this way whenever Kinnaird flew off? Why had he never thought of that before? He had been completely oblivious.

It was true that he had gone stir crazy while confined to bed and room while his leg healed. But, really, once he had been able to walk again and had regained the lost strength in his leg, he had not entirely minded sticking to the palace. It had been no chore at all, seeing Reyes every day. Spending more time tending to his own affairs instead of trusting them almost entirely to his steward.

His favorite part had been traveling into the city to select the flowers of the week, then hunting Reyes down at some point to see how he liked them. He had been ecstatic to see how deeply affected Reyes had been by the tiger lilies. He had hoped they would still mean something, especially with all the trouble clouding their days of late.

So could he give up the work he did? Assuming Rhoten was able to release him from duty, Kinnaird rather thought he could, especially if it meant he would finally, really and truly have Reyes.

He just wished he could finish what he was doing more quickly and fly home to tell Reyes his decision.

Seven

Reyes was tired of worrying and tired of being tired. He wished he could simply deal with the impostor in definitive fashion, but such blood thirsty action had never been his way. His mother had made quite certain of that.

He rubbed his temple, willing away his headache, and tried to focus on his duties.

Striding through the halls, ignoring everyone, he made straight for his office. Rhoten had been in meetings most of the morning and should have had a handful more before lunch, but Reyes had managed to shift enough of them that Rhoten could meet with the twins as he wished.

When Reyes finally reached his office, the twins were already seated and drinking coffee, leaning in close to each other as they quietly conversed. Extended Night had well and truly fallen, making even late morning no different than midnight. The drapes were drawn to block out cold, and the room was aglow with the warm light of fire and lamps.

Reyes nodded in greeting but did not pause as he walked across the room to his desk. He set all his things down, sorting out letters and notes, paperwork he needed to get signed, penning in changes to the week's schedule, shuffling other appointments around. He reached out to refresh the ink in his quill and froze as the back of his hand brushed against the tiger lilies.

He looked at them and frowned. Four days, and

there had been no communication from Kinnaird. That tended to be a good thing, but he wished the fool could be bothered to send *some* word. Bah. Finishing his work, Reyes grabbed his portfolio and went to join Erices and Breit at the table.

"Good morning, Reyes," Breit greeted. "Those are beautiful tiger lilies. I am impressed Kinnaird could get them; even for His Grace, they must be special ordered."

Reyes shrugged, but made mental note to tell Kinnaird yet again to stop being so ridiculously flashy with the flowers. Honestly, he did not need to go to so much effort. Not that Reyes was going to slip up again. He had already said too much in stating that he hated how Kinnaird was simply not around. He would greatly prefer seeing Kinnaird more often to simply looking at expensive flowers.

Erices chuckled. "Kinnaird's father was the same way, if I recall. Always with the extravagant gifts. I daresay your ring will outstrip anything even royalty owns, someday."

"I think we are getting entirely too presumptuous and ahead of ourselves," Reyes said stiffly. "From flowers I constantly tell him to stop bringing, all the way to marriage rings? That is quite the leap, Captain." Breit and Erices only laughed. Reyes ignored them both and focused on his coffee and cake.

A few minutes later Rhoten finally arrived, looking haggard and worn and easily twice his age. Reyes's hands balled into fists in his lap, and it was only with great effort that he managed to force his fingers to uncurl again. "Majesty. You should be free for the next two and a half hours." And if the guards disobeyed his edict to let *no one* in, they would get the full brunt of his temper. Many of them had already learned not to cross the king's secretary. He hoped they remembered the lesson.

"So I see that, to date, we have found no way to rid ourselves of the impostor," Erices said sourly.

Rhoten shook his head and murmured a quiet thanks as he accepted the coffee Reyes held out. "The council is making more and more noise about giving him a chance. He is preferable to Alana and older than she… It all hinges on his having the magic, of course, but I fear by the time he is done, they will not even care about that."

"I do not understand why they like him so much, and more than Dilane, who is by far the more preferable," Breit said.

Reyes sneered. "Everyone loves a scandal. It makes a fine story, you must admit. Keene is powerful, being a distant cousin and so possessing both the fox shift and some measure of the royal magic—but he does not have the tragic story, he is not a guilty secret. Neither does he possess the excessive charm." It made his skin crawl, Gandy's charm, but likely he was just biased against Gandy, not least of all because when it came to charm, he preferred Kinnaird's. Not that he would ever tell Kinnaird that, whatever became of them.

Honestly, he really did hate Gandy, stepping in so selfishly to ruin so many lives just because he thought his birth entitled him to something.

Perhaps it did, to a point. Birthright was important, but at least men like Rhoten and Dilane and Kinnaird had earned their birthrights. Men like Gandy just made him angry. Why could he not be happy with the life he had or earn a better one honestly, without causing so many people to suffer for his selfishness? It was obvious he cared about the crown, not Rhoten. Reyes could not understand it. Some things were far more important than station and power.

He stubbornly ignored the little voice reminding him that same logic applied to himself and Kinnaird. But he would deal with that complication later, after this problem of the bastard had been resolved. Now was entirely the wrong time to work out the issues between himself and Kinnaird.

"I do hope," Breit said not without humor, "that Gandy is the only bastard prince running around. One is already more than we can handle. I do not know what we would do with two or more."

Rhoten grimaced. "Oddly enough, when he said he was my son, he did not name as his mother the woman I had ho—expected."

"Oh?" Erices asked, looking astonished. "Your Majesty has had affairs? You are a damned good secret keeper. Even your secretary looks a bit taken aback."

Reyes rolled his eyes. "I am only responsible for scheduling His Majesty's leisure time—I do not arrange how he spends it. I, at least, appreciate that it is none of my business."

"There were only two," Rhoten said. "Gandy's alleged mother when I was only eighteen. That lasted only the one night. I met another woman a year or so after my marriage at the Extended Day Festival. She was a shop clerk, though she never said as to what manner of shop. Five nights we had together. I spent most of that festival pretending not to be a king." A wistful look flickered across his face. "It was unfortunate we were both already married by that point. I would have taken her to wife and never looked back."

Reyes scowled and poured more coffee. "That would have been extremely risky and foolish. At least you did not take more risks than that."

"The first was quite stupid, I do agree," Rhoten replied. "At eighteen, however, it seemed trifling enough, being just one night. The second was more foolish still, I concede, but I will never regret it. Myra was her name." He smiled, sweet and sad, and sighed softly.

Breit smiled over the rim of his coffee cup. "I am certain she was a fine woman. No doubt if Gandy were her son, he would have turned out a better man. But it is Gandy with whom we must contend. Have we learned anything about the mother?"

Reyes nodded and flipped open his portfolio, setting his coffee aside as he pulled out the letters he had received only a few hours ago. "She is definitely dead, buried in Kria. I've copies of her death certificate, and the village chief wrote a letter telling us what he could. He did say she never mentioned a son, but that she was also an extremely private person who said practically nothing about herself. They lived in a village that was in the general area called the borderlands. That means they were close to Salhara. Otherwise, I fear this is all very much a dead end. We cannot definitively prove him a liar this way."

"Our best chance is to prove he does not possess the royal magic," Erices said, "but he can stall on that indefinitely."

Reyes frowned. "Kinnaird thinks he will use seven-year flower elixir to artificially create it."

"That would take a great deal of skill and one of the higher level elixirs," Breit said with a frown, "and that comes with a great deal of risk. I've never seen it used myself, but I recall Kinnaird's stories of Salhara. They train for years to use it beyond the most basic of spells. Only a small percentage of the country is ever allowed to take any color above blue—that's how they are graded, you see. Violet the lowest, up through indigo, blue, green, yellow, orange, red. You must have a special license for any color above blue, and a very small handful only are allowed to use yellow and higher. The elixir is highly addictive, and dangerous, even fatal, if you take it without training. There are very good reasons Salhara is the only country known to use artificial magic."

"Kinnaird will be able to tell if he is using it," Reyes said, not bothering to mention that Kinnaird had explained the symptoms to him. There was no guarantee he would realize what he was looking at until too late—if at all.

Erices and Breit laughed, so perfectly matched that one could almost have been the mirror of the other. "Yes, Kinnaird certainly made that clear enough, from what I hear. Kinnaird always was the bold sort, though he can occasionally be persuaded toward subtle." Breit glanced at the tiger lilies, mouth curving in a smile. "Not terribly often, though. Hopefully he is too far away for anyone to feel compelled to take his threat seriously."

Reyes's hand jerked, smearing ink across papers. His body went cold with fear. "What do you mean? That someone will attempt to kill him because he has knowledge of seven-year flowers?" He scowled at his ruined notes, so mad at Kinnaird he would not mind cutting loose with his temper one little bit.

He was madder at himself for standing right there on the terrace and letting Kinnaird kiss him senseless, then being so stupidly happy Kinnaird had asked him a favor. He had stood there like a fool—a love struck fool happy to have his lover home—and watched him intimidate Gandy, completely oblivious to the fact Kinnaird had so brazenly put his life in danger.

"Kinnaird will be fine," Rhoten said gently, squeezing Reyes's shoulder. "Do you honestly think he will let anyone kill him after your last conversation?"

He winked.

Reyes scowled. "I think he is a fool. He can do whatever he wants, for all I care." He stabbed viciously at a fresh sheet of paper, then glared at the ruined mess and set the quill aside in favor of his coffee.

"I think they would be fools indeed to kill His Grace after such a confrontation. It would look more than a little suspicious if he suddenly turned up dead." Erices refilled his own coffee and sat back in his seat. "Kinnaird would have known that when he went to face Gandy."

Reyes refused to be soothed. "As I have already said, His Grace can do as he likes."

Though if he came home broken and bleeding again, Reyes did not know what he would do. Never talk to the fool again. Or finish the job. Or, more likely, just worry himself to death because he obviously was not doing enough of that already.

"Reyes—"

He was thankfully spared whatever Breit had to add to the conversation by a knock on the door. Standing, more than willing to snarl at a guard because the fool was several miles away, Reyes yanked the door open. But it was not a guard at the door.

Reyes frowned in confusion at the stranger standing before him. "May I help you?"

The man bowed low, and Reyes noticed he was dressed in somewhat old-fashioned clothing, the sort they still wore up north, in the truly rough regions. "My apologies for disturbing you. I am looking for a Lord Reyes O'Bannon."

"It's just 'Master,'" Reyes replied. "I am Reyes O'Bannon. Who are you?"

"Oh, I'm sorry. My name is Tamark Feythe. I am Steward of Feyestone. I was told that if I could not reach Lord Kinnaird, then I was to speak directly to you."

"Tamark?" Reyes echoed and then the name clicked. "Oh, of course, Baron. I was not expecting you so soon. But please, come in. I've the paperwork on my desk; it can be signed immediately."

"Baron? Oh, no, I am afraid there is some mistake. I am just the Steward."

Rhoten laughed, drawing their attention, beckoning them into the room. "No, I do believe Kinnaird told me to see the current baron stripped of his title and the barony given to you."

Tamark blanched as he realized who was speaking. "Y-Your Majesty," he said, dropping hastily to one knee and bowing his head. "My apologies."

"Oh, you need not apologize. Come and sit with us, my good baron. It is only fitting given your new status."

Slowly standing, Tamark took the seat that Reyes had quickly and neatly cleared of his own things. "I confess I am quite confused, Your Majesty," Tamark said, looking uncomfortable and a little dazed but determined. "I did not know I was being given the title. I came to report what I have learned of the attack on the Northern Treasury as the Duke of Keyes requested. His Grace told me that if I could not find him, I was to speak with Master O'Bannon."

Reyes paused in the middle of gathering the paperwork that Tamark would need to sign to formally take up his new title. "He said that?" Maybe Reyes would let him live after all. Though he was still angry. He lightly touched a tiger lily as he moved around his desk and strode back to the table, setting the paperwork and a pen before Tamark. "May as well take care of everything while you are here, my lord. What did you need to tell me?"

"I did some digging after His Grace left. Had

my son and some trusted men do different digging. We learned Lord Marland often met with a couple of men in one of his favorite whorehouses under guise of them all being visitors. One of the men we could learn nothing about. He was very careful. The other, however, was much more careless. A few of the whores managed to describe him well enough that I was able to sketch this." He reached into his tunic and extracted a smudged piece of heavy drawing paper, which he handed to Reyes.

Unfolding it, Reyes swore softly. "Captain, collect the Earl of Pleasant for questioning."

Erices did not bother asking any questions. He simply stood, retrieved his sword from the back of his chair, and buckled it into place. He paused briefly to grip Breit's shoulder in farewell before striding from the room. Reyes could hear him calling for guards before the door finished closing.

Rhoten looked sadly at the drawing as he took it from Reyes. "A pity. No doubt it was money."

"No doubt," Reyes agreed, thinking of all the taxes owed, the reports he had recently received in regard to the earl's massive gambling debts. Money did it every single time.

Breit frowned. "Reyes. You had best go see my brother. He is in the earl's bedroom. Do not attract attention."

Reyes frowned. "How—" At the look Breit gave him, he stopped and simply nodded, setting his things down on the table before striding from the room.

He moved quickly through the halls, but not with overt urgency. People were used to seeing him rushing about and so paid him no mind. A guard was stationed outside the earl's chambers. When he saw Reyes, he opened the door and motioned for Reyes to precede him then followed him inside and closed and locked the door.

Erices was standing by the bed, and Reyes strode across the room to join him. "Your brother said…" He drifted off as he got a good look at the bed—and the dead Earl of Pleasant spread across it.

"Poisoned," Erices said, voice so mild they might have been discussing the weather, were it not for the thunderclouds in his eyes. "Probably slipped into his brandy, and the poor bastard never woke up. He's lucky he got such a kind poison. A pity we will not be able to string him up for treason." He turned away from the bed. "Someone must have suspected we were close."

Reyes glanced at the bed again, then away. "Or the earl had ceased to be useful."

Erices' brows shot up in surprise. "You are remarkably calm about this for a paper pusher."

"I am peasant born, Captain, and yet made it as far as king's secretary," Reyes replied. "It may surprise you what I have seen and the secrets I have been told to keep." The secrets he kept still and would always keep.

"Point," Erices said, and rested a hand on the hilt of his sword. "We need to figure out what made him useful."

Reyes sighed and pushed at his glasses, wishing it were late enough in the day for a drink, then dismissing the notion. He looked around the room, wrinkling his nose at the lingering scent of cherries and vanilla and something else he could not quite place at the moment. "The Earl of Pleasant owned a small but respectable fleet of merchant ships. He traded primarily in furs, perfumes, other such luxury goods. He was heavily behind in taxes owed on the goods he imported and was about to be brought up on serious charges if he did not pay them in full by end of year. He wouldn't have been able to do it, however, because he had additional gambling debts in excess of three times the value of his estates."

Erices winced. "That is impressive in a sick and awful way. So he clearly needed whatever money was offered him to betray the king—but what did he have that they wanted?"

"I have no way of knowing at present," Reyes replied. "I can have his paperwork in my office by end of day and begin to sort through it, but even if he were stupid enough to put something in writing, finding it will take me some time."

"Likely a dead end, but best do it," Erices said, raking a hand through his hair. "I suppose I had best gather men and go investigate his home. If I see anything of interest, I will see it sent to you with all possible haste."

Reyes nodded, poking around the earl's desk, taking what he could find, but having little hope any of it would prove useful. "I will get started, then. I trust you can see this is dealt with discreetly? I feel his death should not come to light sooner than is strictly necessary."

Erices grunted. "I'll take care of it. Let slip his debts, and I can make sure the impression is that he's run off to hide from creditors. That will buy us a few days' time, and hopefully that will be enough."

"It will be done," Reyes replied and, papers in hand, departed.

When he returned to his office, only Rhoten remained. Reyes saw that Tamark had signed the papers making him the new Baron of Feyestone. Scooping those up with the rest of the papers in his arm, he strode to his desk to begin sorting the mess out.

"So the earl was helping and now he is dead," Rhoten said quietly, playing absently with a sugar spoon.

"Yes," Reyes replied, wondering how he knew already—probably the same way Breit had known Erices needed him, and there was definitely something suspicious about the twins. He had his ideas but surely not. That sort of magic was myth. Bah. He would sort it out later. "I am sorry, Rhoten."

Rhoten sighed and stood up. "Reyes, cancel the rest of my day. If you need me, I shall be in my room, but I have no desire to see anyone else. The servants are to leave my food in the drawing room and come no further than that."

"Yes, Majesty," Reyes said quietly. "Shall I come see you in a bit and read to you?"

"That would be nice," Rhoten replied, managing a weak but genuine smile. "But there is no hurry. Finish up what you must and do not work too hard, Reyes. I hate to see you as exhausted as you are these days."

"Yes, Majesty," Reyes said, returning the smile, ignoring the order to have more care. He did not work half as hard as Rhoten, so there was no damned way he would work even less. Rhoten worried too much about him.

Alone, he extinguished all the lamps but the one on his desk then quickly sorted through the papers, sending the documents for Tamark's new appointment to Baron off for final officiating before focusing on the earl's papers.

Unfortunately, as he had feared, they contained nothing useful. He sent off further requests, with the king's stamps, to order all of the earl's papers released to him. Those he would not have until morning, and with the rest of the king's day canceled…

He hesitated over a blank sheet of paper, mind narrowing to a single sharp, bright thought—Kinnaird.

Reyes should not bother him; Kinnaird was plenty busy in Cassala. On the other hand, he should be kept informed, in case any of it helped his investigation.

Since the bastard could not be bothered to do any writing himself, it would seem Reyes would have to do it. He readied paper and quill and quickly wrote an accounting of recent events, then signed and sealed it.

The back of his hand brushed against the tiger lilies as he strode past his desk to take the letter to the Falcon Master.

Eɪɢʜᴛ

"Good morning, Dilane," Kinnaird greeted.

Dilane nodded sleepily and yawned. He sat at the table and immediately poured coffee, waving off the servant who tried to step forward and do it for him. He drank half the contents of his cup in two gulps. "So what are your plans for the day, my friend? I have seen very little of you these past couple of days. Learn anything?"

"Very little, alas," Kinnaird conceded reluctantly. "However, I am meeting with a friend tonight who hopefully will have additional information for me. Otherwise, the only real thing of value I have learned in the past few days is that someone, more than likely a woman, was here meeting frequently with the late chief. I sense she is largely responsible for the destruction, or at least the arrangement of it. About her, however, I have unfortunately learned nothing more than that she had atrocious taste in perfume."

Dilane grunted and poured a second cup of coffee, drinking it as quickly as he had the first. As he poured a third, however, he began to look more awake. "Well, I assume you will let me know when there is something worth saying."

Kinnaird smirked behind his own coffee cup. "Yes, Highness."

Dilane rolled his eyes. "At least there have been no more attacks—false or otherwise. The bridge recovery proceeds apace." He grinned in amusement.

"A pity we did not bring your little secretary along; he would have this city running smooth as clockwork by now."

Smiling softly, because that was true, Kinnaird replied, "He has his hands full at present, I think. That reminds me—we really should write to let them know how matters proceed." He sipped at his first cup while Dilane polished off his third, silently composing the letter in his head.

Dilane chuckled and began to select food from the various trays upon the table. "You are already quite hopeless, but I suppose you have been for some time, at that. I cannot wait to see how much worse you get when he finally gives in."

"I will do whatever it takes to keep him from changing his mind," Kinnaird muttered, wondering how much in poor taste it would be to give Reyes a ring the same day they became lovers. "Oh, do stop laughing at me."

Dilane smiled. "It is only out of jealousy, really. At least you are able to marry where you please. That is quite the luxury in our world. I should not complain, seeing as my marriage will gain me a crown, but…" He shrugged and said nothing more.

Kinnaird nodded in sympathy, and they fell into a companionable silence until a servant quietly approached with a letter on a silver salver. His name was on it, Kinnaird immediately saw, written in Reyes's hand. Thanking the servant, he took the letter and broke the seal, reading the contents quickly. He swore as he finished.

"What's wrong?" Dilane asked.

Passing the letter to him, Kinnaird said, "The Earl of Pleasant is dead by poison. He was also apparently tied to the attack on the Northern Treasury, which means he could have been involved in any number of the attacks—including this one."

Dilane read the letter, then set it aside. "He sounds afraid, Kinnaird. That is not like your little secretary. He has nerves of steel, could put a hardened veteran to shame."

Not entirely true. Reyes was simply all too good at hiding when things truly upset him. It frightened Kinnaird that someone other than he could read the unspoken fear in Reyes's letter.

"I'm going home," he said abruptly, standing up.

"I'll take care of everything here," Dilane said immediately, not even attempting to argue with him, even if they both knew Kinnaird should stay. "Keep me informed, won't you?"

Kinnaird nodded. "Of course. Though, speaking of informed, if you are to cover for me…" He called for writing supplies and sat down again. "You had best meet with the friend I was going to see tonight, and you will not be allowed to meet him uninvited. Unfortunately, I do not have time to make proper introductions." He thanked the servant who brought the supplies then swiftly wrote a letter to Sharla. He signed it, sealed it with his signet, and handed it to Dilane. "Take this, late tonight, to the Three Moon's Hall. Tell the manager you wish to see *him*. Say that and only that when the manager approaches. Give the manager that letter, and you will be invited up shortly thereafter. When you meet him, be firm and unaffected. He will respect nothing less."

Dilane looked confused, but also faintly amused, as he tucked the letter away. "As you say. Take care of matters back home."

"I intend to," Kinnaird replied and then left, taking his cloak from the club doorman and stepping outside.

Though it was morning, only the mage-lit lanterns interspersed along the streets kept them from being pitch black. It might have been the middle of the night, the stars were so visible, the dark so absolute. Extended Night was more than a little disorienting to strangers, and even those who had lived with it their entire lives found it taxing.

He strode rapidly through the city, all the way to the city gates, past them and well away from the city proper before he finally found a suitable place to shift.

Then he took to the sky, letting out a piercing cry, mind only on Reyes, worried and entirely too unprotected back home.

Pain shot through him, catching him by surprise, and he screamed as he began to fall, the arrow lodged in his left wing making it impossible to fly.

It was also hard to hold on to all his magic—heat shields, his shape, what little healing he could muster to minimize pain. Only the fact he landed in a deep snow drift saved him from the fall itself.

He struggled to focus, to get a grip, but it was so hard to think around the *pain.*

Someone was coming, he could hear the man moving through the snow. Sun and moon damn them all. Who had been bold enough to order his death? But it did mean he had scared someone, as empty as that reassurance was at present. They were willing to risk the suspicion that would rise when the Duke of Keyes suddenly turned up dead.

Damn it.

He needed to change back, but he did not dare with the arrow still in his wing—there was simply no way of knowing where it would remain in his body, or if it would, when he changed back. Shifting was difficult. There were reasons it had taken generations for someone to figure out how to shift with clothes.

The sound of footsteps drew closer, and Kinnaird braced himself to die, hoping that Reyes would not hate him forever, nor mourn him forever.

"Kinnaird!" Sharla said, coming over the mound of snow. She dropped to her knees, carelessly letting go of a bloody sword. "Thank sun and moon. I saw you fall and feared we were too late." Then she carefully picked him up, and Kinnaird resisted an instinctive urge to fight her off. "Brace yourself," she warned, then yanked the arrow from his wing.

Kinnaird cried out in pain, but even as he did so, Sharla was pouring healing magic into him. "Can you change back?"

It took more focus and energy than he liked, but after several minutes Kinnaird at last managed it. As he lay gasping against the lingering pain throbbing in his right side, Dilane came over the rise, clutching a bloody sword of his own and leading a horse. "Thank sun and moon," he said. "I truly thought we were too late."

"What—" Kinnaird swore and gripped his side. It had just been his wing as a bird, but wounds were wildly unpredictable between forms. He was damned lucky he had been smart enough not to change while the arrow remained. "What happened?"

Sharla's mouth tightened, and then she said, "I received word less than an hour ago that a contract has been put out for you—a quarter million sovereigns for the carcass of the Duke of Keyes. I came to you as quickly as I could, but you were already gone. Your friend helped me find you, but we found you just as they shot you down. I am glad we reached you in time."

"I am definitely in your debt, Sharla," Kinnaird replied, forcing himself to his feet. "Dilane. Thank you both."

"Do what I asked, and we shall call it even," Sharla replied, mouth curving in a rare true smile.

Kinnaird returned it. "Of course." He looked her over, dressed in breeches and snow boots, her hair neatly coiled on top of her head, sword belt obviously at home on her hips. He had only ever seen her in gowns, but he wasn't surprised she wore more armor and sword as easily as the gowns. Then he turned to Dilane. "Do you still have that letter I gave you?" He grimaced as he shifted and took the letter when Dilane held it out. Then he gave it to Sharla.

She took it, amused, and quickly read through it. Tucking it away when she finished, she turned to Dilane. "Your Grace—or should I say Your Highness?—it is an honor to make your acquaintance." She dipped into a curtsy elegant enough to put a Duchess to shame.

Kinnaird laughed, then made a show of formal introduction. "Your Highness, I present to you Milady Sharla Klair, Lord of the Cassala Underworld."

Dilane looked surprised for a moment, then simply amused and impressed. He held out his hand, into which Sharla placed hers and kissed the back of it.

He lingered over it, unless Kinnaird was mistaken—and was his mind completely addled by pain, or was Sharla's flush not entirely due to exertion? *That* was interesting.

It was also irrelevant for the moment, so far as he was concerned. "Clearly, I can trust Cassala to your fine hands," he said to both of them. "I must be off."

Dilane broke away from his staring match with Sharla. "Are you strong enough to fly?"

Kinnaird hid a wince as he stretched to test his healed flesh. "Strong enough? I have no idea. Probably not. But I *am* stubborn enough. If whoever is behind all this is willing to pay so much to have me eliminated, he will not hesitate to kill you, Dilane. Take extra precaution."

Such persons would also not hesitate in the slightest to remove a stubborn secretary if they thought him in the way. Kinnaird needed to get home. He would not be satisfied until Reyes was in his arms.

Ignoring the worried looks of the other two, he began to draw his power together. "Dilane, help me launch."

"Of course," Dilane replied.

Gritting his teeth, biting back cries of pain, Kinnaird shifted. It left him reeling and nauseated, and he half-wondered if something had been added to the arrow, but he could do nothing about that until he was home. So home he would go.

When he had at last shifted, Dilane knelt and Kinnaird hopped onto his arm. When Dilane stood and threw his arm up, Kinnaird launched himself into the air. He cried out in thanks and farewell then put all his energy into getting home as quickly as possible.

The journey seemed to take three times longer than normal. Rather than the terrace, he flew straight to Reyes's office, alighting on the small balcony and letting out a piercing cry. A heartbeat later, the balcony door slammed open and Reyes—exhausted, strained, but unmistakably happy to see him—appeared.

Kinnaird pushed off the railing and shifted, landing inside on the floor. He stood up, said Reyes's name, and then promptly passed out.

~~*

He woke with a mild headache, recognizing it as a side-effect of being struck with a great deal of magic. Healing, likely, especially if he had been poisoned as he suspected. That on top of flying so soon after being grievously wounded… He really was lucky to be alive.

Sitting up, he realized he was in his bedroom. Well, where else would they have put him? Honestly. Shaking his head, immediately regretting it as the headache flared up, he glanced around and realized he was not alone. His heartbeat kicked up several notches as he took in the sight of Reyes, beautifully lit by the firelight, as he sat at a table in front of it, diligently bent over paperwork.

"Good morning," Kinnaird said, guessing as to the time of day, unable to tell from his bed.

Reyes jerked, pen slashing ink across the paper on which he had been writing. He looked up and glared at Kinnaird, then looked back at his papers.

"Nothing to say?" Kinnaird asked, a bit stung that Reyes seemed to have absolutely nothing to say, nor even seem inclined to come at least look at him. But it was silly to be hurt, and he knew that.

"I'm not speaking to you," Reyes said flatly, not looking up.

"Ah," Kinnaird replied, relief curling through him. "Why ever not?"

"Because I hate you," Reyes snapped, ruining another sheet of paper, swearing colorfully as he cast it aside and drew a fresh sheet toward him.

It was completely the wrong time to smile, but Kinnaird did so anyway. "Reyes, come here."

"No."

"Come here or I will walk over there."

"You will stay in that damned bed, or I will finish the job of killing you!" Reyes snarled, voice breaking slightly on the last two words.

"Then come here," Kinnaird said quietly. "Please."

Reyes slammed his quill and papers down, then shoved his chair back and strode across the room. He hovered near the bed, but not quite close enough for

Kinnaird to touch. Not unless...

He lunged, grabbing Reyes about the waist, twisting at the last moment so that they wound up sprawled and tangled on the bed.

"This is not making me hate you any less," Reyes hissed, the angriest Kinnaird had ever seen him.

"No," Kinnaird agreed. "Probably not, but it makes it a good sight easier to start making you not hate me again."

Reyes only continued to glare. "You are welcome to try, but I do not anticipate you having much success."

More than willing to accept the invitation and the challenge, Kinnaird kissed him. He only got his lip bitten, but he considered it a price worth paying when Reyes began to feverishly kiss him back. He did not relent until Reyes was clinging to him and shaking in his arms.

"I'm sorry," he murmured when he finally drew back. "I did not mean to worry you. I thought I was sufficiently healed to make it here without doing something as dramatic as collapsing."

Reyes's eyes slid shut. "Your wound reopened. There was blood everywhere. You were also poisoned nearly to death. It was all I could do to keep you alive long enough for the healers to reach you."

Kinnaird winced. "I'm sorry. I truly had no idea it was so bad." He kissed Reyes's mouth again, his cheeks, his nose, peppering his face and throat with a mix of soft and hard kisses until some of Reyes's tension finally bled away. "I'm sorry," he finally said a third time. "I got your letter and came straight home. I was shot down barely after I had taken flight—"

"What!" Reyes said, holding so tightly that his nails bit painfully into Kinnaird's arms. "You're a stupid, reckless fool. That letter was just to inform—

and it's your own fault for provoking— I really do *hate* you."

Kinnaird kissed him again, pulling Reyes's hands free and pinning them to the bed, straddling him so that Reyes could go nowhere anytime soon.

"Let me go," Reyes said, but his attempt at anger came out more like petulance.

"No," Kinnaird replied, kissing him again, then trailing kisses along his jaw, down the line of his throat, until cloth kept him from going further. "I came home because you sounded afraid, and I was scared you would be killed next. I did not mean to get shot; it never occurred to me they would do something so reckless. I never meant to frighten you."

He kissed Reyes properly, slow and long, until he had no choice but to pull away for breath. He nibbled at Reyes's jaw, the soft skin he would never cease to admire, and said, "I swear to sun and moon, Reyes, if you want me to stay home I will—so long as you swear to hate me forever."

Reyes jerked in surprise and stared at him for a long moment. "I can't seem to stop, no matter how hard I try."

Kinnaird laughed shakily, relieved and overjoyed, and freed one of Reyes's hands so he could put his own to work stripping away Reyes's clothing.

"You should be resting," Reyes protested, though it turned into a soft, pleased noise as Kinnaird's hand skimmed along his smooth chest.

"Mmm, you can rest with me after I'm done," Kinnaird murmured, as thrilled by the idea of having Reyes sleeping alongside him as he was about finally having Reyes naked in his bed and at his mercy. He cast shirt and jacket aside then put his mouth to one nipple, lapping at it, then biting down. Reyes shivered and moaned, and Kinnaird repeated the touches on the other nipple, eager for more sounds. "You are far sweeter a reality, my dear. Fantasy does not compare, even my very thorough ones."

"Shut up," Reyes muttered and grabbed his hair, dragging Kinnaird down for a hard, dizzying kiss.

Kinnaird groaned and gave as good as he got, mouth as eager to devour as his hands were to explore. He broke away and finally got rid of the last of Reyes's clothes, then took Reyes's cock firmly in hand, touching, exploring, before finally beginning to firmly stroke. He bit down on Reyes's throat and said, "I do wish I had the energy to take you. This will have to do for now."

"It would serve you right—" Reyes bit out "—to die trying—" But he wrapped his own hand around Kinnaird's cock, stroking in time with Kinnaird's motions, until the world narrowed to panting and pleading, slick, sweaty skin, and Kinnaird at last seeing how Reyes looked finding his pleasure.

They collapsed together in a sweaty, sticky heap, and Kinnaird tried to think of something witty to say, but he was fast asleep before he could form the words.

~~*

When he woke again, he was smiling, but it slipped away as he realized he was alone. Had Reyes changed his mind? Was he having second thoughts? Were they going to have to pretend—

Then he saw the single tiger lily where it had slipped off Reyes's pillow to lie in the folds of the blankets.

Smile restored, Kinnaird picked the flower up and climbed out of bed. He was reaching for the bell pull when he saw that Reyes had already had a bath brought. His smile turned into a full grin then, and he hurried to get cleaned and dressed so that he could hunt down Reyes.

An hour later, he strode to the place Reyes could most likely be found—his office.

Unfortunately, Reyes was not the only one in his office—Rhoten and the twins were at the table, just beginning to settle down to lunch. Their presence might have curbed some of his behavior, but it did not stop him from crossing the room to the bookcases where Reyes was putting things away and drawing Reyes in for a sound kiss.

Reyes shoved him back after a startled moment, red-faced and furious. "Behave! This—this is neither the time nor the place. The impropriety!"

Grinning, Kinnaird returned the tiger lily he had brought with him, then strode to his seat at the table and helped himself to the wine.

"You are remarkably recovered for a man who nearly died in this very room only a day and a half ago," Erices said dryly.

Kinnaird only smiled demurely and said, "Thank you. I obviously received the best possible treatment." His smile only widened at the way Reyes rolled his eyes, still shoving books back into place.

"Somehow, I doubt all of that healing was healer-sanctioned," Breit said, laughing into his wine glass.

"It is a good thing, then, that we did not ask," Kinnaird said.

"Oh, for love of sun and moon!" Reyes snapped, slamming a book down. "I do believe we are here to discuss *business*, and it is certainly serious enough a matter that such crass levity is more than a little misplaced, don't you think?"

Kinnaird frowned. That was excessively harsh.

Reyes must still be upset, never mind how frayed he had been to begin with. He was all but coming apart at the seams, but even with all that, this seemed an overreaction. "What is wrong? Did something else happen while I was asleep?"

"It has filtered back here to Basden that His Majesty gave Dilane the royal ring. People are getting extremely heated debating the matter," Breit said.

"They are being buffoons about it," Reyes said tersely, shoving in the last few books, then striding to his desk to begin subjecting paperwork to his foul mood—though he was nothing but gentle as he first carefully restored the tiger lily to the bouquet.

Hiding a smile, Kinnaird said, "Well, they can debate until they are blue in the face, but let us face it— whatever people want, whatever they say, it is His Majesty alone who can say 'yes, you are my son.' The marriage contracts between Dilane and Her Highness have been signed for years. The wedding takes place the beginning of next year. Dilane is only a few months and a ceremony away from legally being Crown Prince. If he chooses to take up the role of Acting Crown Prince, he is within his rights, so long as the king grants permission—which he has. Let them blather on, I say."

Erices grunted in agreement. "At least your dramatic arrival distracted them for a time. How is Dilane?"

"Too alone for my liking," Kinnaird replied. "Whoever is behind this put up a quarter million sovereigns to have me killed. They nearly succeeded. I was going to suggest that you go and look after him, as I trust no one else more."

"We'll both go," Breit said before Erices could speak.

Rhoten nodded, deciding the matter. "Please, do. Now that Kinnaird is here, he can help us address the matter of Gandy. I grow tired of this matter and would like to see it ended. Protect my heir in the meantime. Kinnaird came far too close to death for my taste. I do not want to hear of further tragedies or near tragedies."

"Majesty," the twins said in chorus, then stood and bowed in unison, abandoning their lunches to see his orders immediately carried out.

When they were gone, Reyes finally sat down at the table and fidgeted with a glass of wine. "So what do we do now?"

"You tell me what you know, and I will tell you what I learned in Cassala, and together we will see what pieces of this puzzle we are still missing."

Nodding, Reyes went to fetch his portfolio, looking happier with something definitive to do.

Later, Kinnaird thought with a brief burst of happiness, he could drag Reyes away to their bed and make him forget it all for a little while. When Reyes turned, Kinnaird caught his eyes and smiled—and felt happier still when Reyes briefly returned it.

NINE

Reyes was losing his mind. He had the sinking feeling he had already lost it. He just wanted everything to return to normal—Rhoten happy and not hiding in his room more often than not, Gandy nowhere about, Dilane the definitive heir, and Kinnaird still at a comfortable and *safe* distance.

Argh, why had he surrendered? It was the last damned thing he should have done.

Sun and moon, he had thought it was bad enough when Kinnaird had shown up with his leg badly broken. He had not known what to do when Kinnaird had collapsed in his office two days ago, bleeding to death and seizing from the effects of the poison. It was a miracle he was alive.

Reyes buried his face in one hand, giving up any pretense of doing paperwork. How was he supposed to focus on appointments and meetings when he could not even figure out how to get Rhoten out of his room anymore? He had never seen Rhoten so depressed, and it was only making people like Gandy more powerful—and the whole awful cycle just made him want to lose his temper with every last one of the bastards who would so mistreat Rhoten this way when he had done nothing to deserve it.

He scowled at his portfolio then shoved it away and strode to yank the bell pull to summon a servant. Maggie arrived a couple of minutes later, and he dredged up a smile for her as he asked for wine. Though she looked concerned, Maggie only curtsied and left to get the wine.

Alone again, Reyes pushed away from his desk and paced restlessly, finally pausing at the bookcase, looking at the books without really seeing them. It was all a great big mess, and they had so far found no real way of cleaning it up.

What *did* they know so far? Precious little. The attacks and Gandy were clearly connected; Pleasant alone seemed to prove that, given his connections to Cassala and Feyestone, as well as his remarkably quick friendship with Gandy. There was also the little matter of his death by poison.

Since Cassala, the attacks had stopped, but then, nothing more was really needed, was it? News of all the attacks were filtering back to Basden, flooding the palace with speculation of poor protection, unpreparedness on the part of the royal army, and look at the final cost, they exclaimed—poor Cassala, and how had the king let all this happen?

Meanwhile, Gandy continued to shine and shine, winning friends as people added the scandal of a bastard to all the attacks and tragedy. Reyes hid in his office more than usual simply because if he saw the bastard, he would do something regrettable.

The only lead they had was that two people—a man and a woman—seemed to be orchestrating everything. Why? Did it tie back to Galand or some other country? Who in the name of sun and moon were the two orchestrating it all? Would they ever figure it out?

It made him sick to think about all the places that were attacked, the way they were attacked. Someone with power and authority was selling out Elamas. Someone who had access to the royal palace and likely was laughing at them even now from just a few rooms away.

Reyes curled his hands into fists and struggled to remind himself that nothing would be gained by losing his temper.

Maggie came with the wine then, and he forced himself to turn and smile and chat with her for a little while. If she conveyed he was in good spirits, that was a little less fuel on the fire.

When she was gone, he poured himself a glass of the dark red wine and took a sip, determined to calm down and stop falling apart at the seams. It was amazing to him Kinnaird, the notorious King's Falcon, saw something appealing in someone so fragile as Reyes was clearly proving to be.

Kinnaird…

Fear and irritation still clouded his thinking where Kinnaird was concerned, but there was no denying he mostly felt warm and happy. He was stupid to give in, stupid to take the risk, but he had liked falling asleep next to Kinnaird and waking up beside him.

There were certainly no complaints about the sex, either, even if he was a bit sore today. Flushing, Reyes gulped his wine and tried to find thoughts that were neither brooding nor wildly inappropriate. Wine in hand, he strode back to his desk and sat down—right as someone knocked on the door. "Come in," Reyes called and was surprised to see Vallen, Princess Alana's guardian, step inside. "Can I help you?"

Vallen sketched a polite bow, then said, "Master O'Bannon. Her Highness would like to speak with her father, but all attempts were rebuffed. The guards said that all requests must go through you, regardless of the identity of the requestor." His tone dripped with disapproval that Alana must schedule a time via secretary in order to see her own father.

Reyes ignored the tone, and its unspoken words, and nodded, pulling his ledger out and flipping it open to appointments. "His Majesty is not feeling well and will receive only a small number of visitors per day." To minimize the chances someone might try to hurt him, since there was no telling who else their unseen enemy wanted dead by the end of the mess. "All those wishing to see him will not gain admittance without written approval from me." He dipped his quill in ink and asked, "Why does Her Highness wish to speak with her father?"

"I beg your pardon, Master O'Bannon," Vallen said stiffly, "but if Princess Alana desires to speak with her *father,* then I feel that is all which need concern you."

"My orders were explicit," Reyes replied, unmoved. "The last time Her Highness had words with His Majesty, she did nothing but upset him further. He is not well. I will not see that state exacerbated, per the instructions of the healers and the fact that I am loyal to him before I am loyal to her." He hated Alana, and that was really all the reason he needed, but it was not a terribly professional reason. Eventually he would have to give in, because she was Rhoten's daughter, but he could irritate them first. "I am afraid that if she wishes to speak with him, I will need good reason to authorize it."

"Reconciliation," Vallen replied, biting the words out. "We all know how strained their relationship is, but even Her Highness is deeply frightened that with all the upheaval of late, something terrible will happen to her father. It has scared her into wanting a true reconciliation, to assure him that she is on his side, whatever their differences."

Barely keeping back a sneer, because he believed that not in the slightest, Reyes nevertheless conceded defeat and began to pen the letter of permission—but he added a note for the guards that they were to see she left after fifteen minutes. "Very well," he said tersely, as he finished penning the letter. He signed his name, stamped his seal beside it, then sealed the letter and pressed his personal stamp into the wax. Then he slid it across the desk and said, "Present this to the guards at the half dusk bells. No sooner, no later. If the note is in any way tampered with, she will be refused admittance and must come to me for a new appointment. Is that clear?"

"Quite clear," Vallen replied, and with a stiff bow, took his leave.

Reyes wrinkled his nose when he was alone, irritated by Vallen, Princess Alana, and the noxious mix of cologne and perfume left behind to remind Reyes of them both. Some people should not be allowed to pick out their own scents. Cherries, he thought, and something excessively musky in the cologne. Horrible combination.

He was distracted from his thoughts by the opening of his door, but immediately relaxed as Kinnaird slipped inside and quietly closed the door again. "Good afternoon," Kinnaird greeted.

Sun and moon, he looked good. He always did, of course, but with memories of the previous night still fresh in mind, Reyes only found him that much more attractive. "Kinnaird. What brings you here? Surely there are things you should be doing." He stood up and moved around his desk, briefly reaching out to touch the vivid purple lisianthus that had been on the corner of his desk that morning, arranged in a red crystal vase.

Kinnaird snorted softly in amusement and strode across the room, and then Reyes abruptly found himself pinned to his desk, a thigh shoved between his legs, and he barely caught Kinnaird's murmured, "I needed to kiss you," before his mouth was taken in a very thorough, extremely inappropriate kiss.

"Stop doing such things in my office," Reyes said when Kinnaird finally let him breathe. "What if someone were to walk in?"

"They would either leave again or stay and enjoy the view."

Reyes glared at him, and with a laugh and a quick, biting kiss, Kinnaird let him go, though he remained indecently close. "I came to see how you were doing, and if anyone was making your life particularly difficult."

"Only you," Reyes retorted, but even as he spoke, he obligingly tilted his head to give Kinnaird's mouth better access to his throat.

Kinnaird chuckled, breath warm against Reyes's skin. "Do you like the flowers?"

"Yes," Reyes said on a soft moan, hazily remembering he had told Kinnaird to stop doing this sort of thing in his office. "You do not have to keep giving me flowers, you know. They seem to be a bit pointless now, surely."

Kinnaird paused, making Reyes frown. He looked up with a fond, amused smile. "You mean now I have you? One has nothing to do with the other, my dear. I buy the flowers to make you happy, to see you smile. They still serve that purpose, hmm?"

"Hopeless," Reyes replied, failing entirely to put any sting into the word.

A sudden burst of raucous laughter from the hall made them both freeze in surprise. Mood effectively ruined, Kinnaird stole a last kiss and then stepped far enough away to avoid temptation. "How is Rhoten?"

"The kingdom is questioning his fitness to wear the crown, he no longer knows what to believe himself, a fake son is stealing all the support, and his only daughter is going to be bothering him in a quarter bell. How do you think he is doing?"

Kinnaird made a face. "We will work it out, Reyes. I promise. We are close, I know it."

"I hope so," Reyes said tiredly, worried sick about Rhoten, hating, loathing, despising all those who had put him in such a terrible state. "He doesn't deserve this, not with all he has gone through, all he has endured. Why can they not simply leave him alone?"

Stepping close again, Kinnaird tugged him into a loose embrace. "Because they are fools. Once we find definitive proof Gandy is a shameless liar, you will see them turn on him and claim they never believed it for a single moment. It is the way with people."

Reyes nodded, reassured despite himself, and wondered how long he could stay right where he was before someone finally forced him back to work. As Kinnaird did not seem inclined to let him go, he did not bother to ask.

A familiar series of knocks made him start, and he stared in surprise as the door opened to admit Breit, followed by Dilane, then Erices.

Dilane, alarmingly, looked exhausted and entirely too pale, and he favored his right arm.

"What happened?" Kinnaird asked, letting go of Reyes and striding to Dilane's side, helping him to sit down in a chair.

"Two attempts were made on his life in Cassala," Erices replied. "After the second, we left. We were attacked twice more on our way home." He sat down in the first available chair he reached and ran his hands through his hair. To judge by the state of his clothes, the dried blood on them, he had been injured himself at some point, though the wounds had been healed. "It was risky, leaving Cassala, but we felt it more dangerous to stay."

Kinnaird swore and abruptly left. Reyes moved to his desk, quickly writing notes and yanking the appropriate bell pulls, dispatching them as runners appeared. The guard would be raised across the palace, and Kinnaird had gone off to speak personally with the guards stationed at the king's rooms.

Dilane stirred from where he was all but asleep in his seat. "Can I have some of that wine?" he asked, then frowned as he looked around the room. "Where is Sharla?"

Reyes immediately poured the wine and took it to him. "Who is Sharla?"

"She is a good friend of Kinnaird's," Dilane replied, nodding in thanks for the wine, mouth quirking at some private amusement. "I have only recently made her acquaintance myself."

Reyes frowned, wondering what was so funny.

"She should be along shortly," Erices replied. "I do believe she was actually nervous about meeting His Majesty. I did not know a woman like that could *be* nervous."

Before Reyes could demand better explanations, a series of soft knocks came at the door. Before he could reach it, however, the door opened and Kinnaird stepped through, speaking with someone, then he turned and bowed in the unseen speaker.

As she stepped into the room and pushed back the deep hood of her cloak, Reyes couldn't help but stare a moment before he caught himself. She was the most beautiful woman he had ever seen. Sun and moon, after Kinnaird, she was probably the most beautiful person he had ever seen.

This was a *friend* of Kinnaird's? A good friend?

It was, he reminded himself furiously, completely the wrong time and place for jealousy—not that he would give in to something as petty and weak and ridiculous as jealousy.

"Sharla," Kinnaird said, taking her hand and kissing the knuckles briefly. "It is good to see you again, and so soon after our last parting. I believe you know everyone here, save—"

"You must be Reyes," Sharla said, cutting Kinnaird off, stepping forward to clasp Reyes's hands in her own. Something like understanding flashed across her face, and she continued, "I knew you the moment I saw you from one thousand descriptions." She winked at him. "It was quite distressing to hear him talk and talk about you and pay no mind whatsoever to my meticulously arranged décolletage."

Reyes laughed, the knots in his stomach unwinding. "He can be abysmally rude, I know. I apologize on his behalf."

"Accepted," Sharla replied graciously. "I do not suppose I might have a bit of that wine?"

"Of course," Reyes replied and poured it for her.

Kinnaird looked between them, brows furrowed in confusion and mild annoyance. "Why do I have the distinct impression that I was about to be in a great deal of trouble and now I am not?"

"I have no idea," Reyes replied, tone moderately sharp. "Is His Majesty all right?"

"Yes," Kinnaird replied. "I do not suppose the lot of you have brought us any further information?"

"Some, actually," Sharla said, sitting down next to Dilane, crossing her legs. She was wearing breeches and a sword, and looked quite comfortable with both. "I must say, I have never dealt with such intrigue, not even in my unique social circles."

That begged the question of what her circles were, but a slight shake of the head from Kinnaird said he would get answers later.

"Anyway, I obtained—at great cost—a description of the man who ordered the assassinations of Kinnaird and Dilane. Tall, very broad and muscular, dark hair, has a military bearing."

"We also received reports of strange behavior from some of the merchants about certain Galand traders not renewing contracts, sort of... withdrawing. This time of year, with the fiscal quarter wrapping up, that's more than a little strange."

Reyes frowned, then turned and went to his desk, shuffling papers until he found what he sought. "I have received word of the same thing; I was going to bring it to His Majesty's attention this evening. It seemed strange, but merchants acting strange is seldom news."

"Unless they had good reason to stall. Or thought they did," Kinnaird said. "If they thought the winds of fortune would soon be drastically changing."

"As if we did not know those land-locked rats had something to do with all of this," Erices said with a sneer, then winced as he shifted in his seat. Reyes wondered what manner of wound he had taken that Erices' own healing abilities were insufficient to completely mend it. Breit reached out and lightly touched Erices' leg, then let his hand rest there as Erices unconsciously leaned into him.

"I am a lot more interested in learning more about the rats right in our midst," Kinnaird said. "None of this could have happened without inside help. And the only clue we have is a woman who favors a sickly-sweet perfume."

Sharla laughed, sharp and bright. "That really does not help at all, does it? Just passing through the halls, I was assaulted with the noxious perfumes of girls with more scent than sense. I was freshening up in the powder room and a woman who informed me in ringing tones that she was the princess, not 'my lady', was wearing something more suited to a child—cherry, vanilla, and honey. So I am afraid that scent alone—"

She was drowned out by the crash and tinkle of breaking glass. Everyone turned sharply to look at Reyes, but he ignored them, mind racing. "Sun and moon—the earl's room and my office before, honey! That was the scent I could not catch. Cherry and vanilla and honey. Alana. And she has gone to see him!"

He stopped wasting time talking and bolted, throwing open his office door and tearing through the halls, running as fast as he possibly could. He ignored stares, cries, demands—he ignored everything but getting to Rhoten as quickly as possible.

Surely Alana would not kill her father, he must be panicking—but Reyes would rather be a fool than let something awful happen for fear of being a fool.

He reached the stairs to the king's private wing and took them three at a time. He tripped halfway up, falling down hard, but picked himself up and started running again, ignoring any and all pain.

It all fit, damn her. Alana had been to each of those locations in the past year, staying at each for a month or so before declaring it detrimental to her health, or boring, or whatever. No one would take notice or care if she suddenly popped in again—if they even recognized her. Princess Alana had always kept herself secluded.

The description of the man offered by Sharla matched Vallen. That made sense. Who better to have as an accomplice than her own guardian?

He reached Rhoten's rooms and snarled for the guards to let him inside. They immediately obeyed, but Reyes scarcely noticed their wide-eyed looks as he raced past them.

"Get away from him," he snarled, seeing Alana skulking near her father, Gandy and Vallen leaning over him, pinning him in his chair. The king's mouth bled from where he had obviously been struck. "Get away!" he repeated, charging toward them.

Alana scowled and threw up her hand, focusing her destructive energy at him, releasing it even as the king bellowed for her not to do it.

Reyes reacted a split second too late, throwing up his shields only enough to block the worst of it, the remaining force sending him crashing back into a washstand. It rocked hard into the wall, sending the bowl and pitcher on top tumbling off. Reyes threw up his arm to keep it all from smashing on his head, managing instead to only get doused in soapy water.

He paid it no mind, instead scrambling to his feet and this time better prepared as Alana readied for another attack. Glaring, she lifted her hand—then snapped around and faced Rhoten.

"Leave. Him. Alone!" Reyes bellowed, throwing his own power at her, letting it go, holding nothing back. Too late he recalled himself and remembered just how destructive that much power would be. Why he had kept it completely dormant for more than ten years.

When he could finally see clearly again, rather than though a haze of fear and anger, it was to find that Alana, Gandy, and Vallen were all dead. Likely they had very few bones left which were not broken, if any.

Rhoten stared at him, wide-eyed and disbelieving. "Reyes—"

As the full impact of his mistake struck him, Reyes dropped to his knees and buried his hands in his hair.

"Sun and moon," Erices swore, and his voice was immediately followed by the slamming and locking of the doors, and Reyes felt ill to realize they were no longer alone. "Did His Majesty kill them, then?"

"No," came Kinnaird's voice, and Reyes flinched as he realized that Kinnaird had seen everything—something about that soft tone told him that his secret was no longer a secret. "Not Rhoten."

Reyes heard him coming but could not make himself move. He was frozen with fear and dread, the weight of his terrible mistake—three people dead and his secret uncovered, and why in the name of sun and moon had he let himself lose control? He had *promised,* and he had never wanted anyone to *know.*

He was shaking hard as Kinnaird pulled his hands free, keeping firm hold of them as he gently tugged Reyes to his feet. Reyes stared miserably at the costly hair dye staining his hands, recalling the soapy water that had poured over him. A soft spell wash over him, warm and tingling, as Kinnaird removed the dye entirely. He could not bear to look up, to see their faces—Rhoten's, Kinnaird's. What would he see in their faces?

"The king did not kill them," Kinnaird repeated and grasped Reyes's chin, forcing his head up. He gently removed Reyes's glasses and tossed them aside, then softly added, "The prince did."

Reyes closed his eyes, unable to bear the looks of shock as they all finally realized his secret.

"Sun and moon," Dilane muttered. "Right in front of our damned noses this entire time—for years, even!"

"Myra," Rhoten said. Reyes's eyes snapped open, dismayed to hear Rhoten crying, and he started to apologize, but drew up short when he realized Rhoten was smiling, if a trifle shakily. "You are Myra's son. Myra and I had a son— I—" He started crying too hard to speak and instead settled for pulling Reyes into a tight embrace.

Shaking, Reyes held just as tightly, feeling too many things of a sudden to even begin to sort them all out. He had no idea what to do now he was free of all pretense. After a few minutes, Rhoten finally drew back and touched Reyes lightly in wonder—the golden hair, the pale brown eyes. They had the same cheekbones, but his nose, chin and mouth all came from his mother.

"I cannot believe…" Rhoten whispered. "This whole time… and no one ever realized. Not even the sharp eyes of a smitten falcon. Why the secrecy, Reyes? Oh, sun and moon, you are my son—really and truly my son." He hugged Reyes tightly again, laughing and crying.

When Reyes was finally let go, all the words he could never say came tumbling out in a rush. "Mother made me promise never to tell, and I did not want to cause trouble or upset anyone. It was never about being a prince to me. Mother loved you. She did not want to burden you or ruin other lives. She— I always wanted to see you, just once. I became a secretary because it seemed the surest way for the son of a bookshop clerk to reach the palace and be well-placed to see you. I-I never thought I would wind up your personal secretary. W-when I did, it was enough for me that I got to be so close to you. I-I-I never planned to tell anyone, e-even if of l-late I have come to accept that one person would have to know."

He wanted badly to look at Kinnaird but was too terrified of what he would see. "I'm sorry," he said at last, shoulders sagging. "I should not have lost control, but when I realized Alana was the traitor, all I could think was that they were going to hurt m-m-my f-father."

The words ended on a sob, and he had not realized until that moment just how very badly he had always wanted to address Rhoten so—how much he had wanted to say that one simple word.

Rhoten embraced him again, still laughing and crying. "A son, a son, Myra and I have a son."

"Had," Reyes said, brief happiness dying. "Mother died several years ago, shortly before I left to come to Basden. I'm sorry."

"I think I knew, or convinced myself she had," Rhoten said sadly. "I do wish… a lot of things, but they will never come to pass now. But we have a son, and I am very happy for that." He cupped Reyes's face in one hand and shook his head. "It seems so plain, now. I cannot believe I never saw her in you."

"Mother disguised my appearance from the time I was a babe," Reyes replied. "She made certain I kept it up, even when I protested, until I was at last old enough to be told the truth. Then I understood and maintained it myself." He smiled. "She told me stories about you, all that she could find, all she knew. They were my favorite. When she finally told me the truth… that is why I wanted so badly to meet you."

"Incredible," Erices said.

"As much as I am loath to break up this reunion," Sharla said, "we have serious problems on our hands—namely, a dead princess and two other corpses."

"No," Kinnaird said suddenly, making Reyes jump. "We have three corpses. Majesty, I am sorry, but I fear that to salvage this situation, we must hide that your daughter is dead."

Rhoten looked sad. "I never… It is a shameful thing to admit, but it was always hard to think of her as my daughter. I tried. So many times I tried. No doubt it is unfair of me; perhaps I see too much of her mother in her… She betrayed me, however, and our kingdom. Do what you must, Kinnaird, and I will do my part."

Kinnaird moved away from them, though Reyes thought that he felt fingers brush softly across his back. He hoped he was not imagining it. Then Kinnaird stood in the center of the room, immediately commanding attention. "Then here is what we are going to do so that this tragedy does not wreak havoc on our kingdom or further trouble our king.

"So far as history will be concerned, Princess Alana came to see her father, accompanied by her guardian and the bastard prince. The king revealed he knew for a fact, and had proof, that Gandy's claims were false. Gandy refused to believe it, and they got into an argument that spiraled out of control. In the end, Gandy tried to kill the king and princess. Vanell died in the ensuing fight before the king finally killed Gandy. With Princess Alana to corroborate, no one will question the matter. If nothing else, they will love the scandal too much to look into it further."

"You seem to be forgetting that you do not have a princess," Sharla said.

Kinnaird smirked, and Reyes smiled faintly, knowing what Kinnaird was thinking, loving seeing him in his element. "No, I have not forgotten. As of today, Your Highness, all our debts are settled."

Sharla stared at him, confused—then her jaw dropped. "But— Kinnaird— I'm— For love of sun and moon, have you gone *mad?* I'm no princess."

"I think you will make for a better one, honestly. You certainly can't do worse than the woman who just tried to murder her own father."

"No one will ever believe it," Sharla replied. "That is far too great a deception."

"They'll believe it," Reyes said. "People see what they expect to see. So they will see a daughter, reclusive her entire life, shaken badly by nearly being killed, by nearly seeing her father killed, by seeing her long-time guardian die. They will see her changed by the tragedy. If the king says you are his daughter, and Dilane says you are his betrothed, who is to say otherwise? We can help you with the details, especially I, for I knew her schedule and habits better than practically anyone else.

Sharla shook her head. "I need to sit down." She strode to the chair vacated by the king and did precisely that, but Reyes could see that she was already turning everything over in her mind, calculating, adjusting.

"I will tend to the bodies," Erices said and strode across the room. "They will have to be completely burned. I am sorry, Your Majesty."

Rhoten's face tightened as he stood up and slowly made his way across the room, waving Erices back. Kneeling before his daughter, he touched her face and said something that did not carry to the rest of the room. Then he rose and motioned for Erices to proceed.

Sharla stood as well. "I am going to need her clothing, her jewelry, everything. Her hair is darker than mine, too, hmm."

Reyes laughed faintly, too overwhelmed and disbelieving not to laugh. "A bit of my hair dye, watered down, should give you the right gold tone for short term, and we can work out long term later."

Nodding, Sharla helped Erices with the bodies, and soon they were gone, sneaking away into the night out Rhoten's balcony doors.

Rhoten sat down. "My new daughter seems interesting, but I think it probably for the best I do not know the finer points of what seems to be her very colorful upbringing. Dilane, are *you* all right with this? It is she who will rule alongside you as queen, she who will be your bride, may sun and moon forgive us for what we do this night."

"I do not mind," Dilane said quietly. "She will make a fine queen."

Rhoten nodded then slid his eyes back to Reyes. The weary expression eased into one of happiness, still tinged with disbelief. "So what are we to do with you, then?"

"Nothing," Reyes replied. "I have no designs on the throne, or on being a prince, or any such thing. All I wanted was to see you. It was the greatest moment of my life to meet you. Now I spend the greater part of every day with you. I am happy being your secretary."

"Then my secretary you shall remain," Rhoten replied, "but you are not allowed to call me Rhoten any longer when we are alone." Reyes frowned, confused. "You must call me Father."

Looking down to hide the sudden sting in his eyes, Reyes smiled softly and said, "Yes, Father."

Rhoten grunted. "Good. Now, let us see if we can salvage this tragic mess and put my kingdom back in order. I am certain I do not need to emphasize that what happened tonight never leaves this room and goes with us to our graves."

"Yes, Majesty," everyone chorused as they all set to work weaving a deception.

TEN

Kinnaird yawned as he walked through the halls, shifting his burden to one arm to scrub tiredly at his eyes. He should have come straight home, but it was the week's beginning, and if he had gone straight to bed he would not have woken up in time to beat Reyes to the office.

Reyes…

They had been so busy the past several days he had scarcely had time to properly think about his lover. It had been days since he had even *seen* Reyes.

First, there had been the bodies. In the end, Erices and Sharla had struck upon the idea of switching the two women completely. Now all of those in Cassala who had known Sharla thought her dead, and Sharla would now forever be Princess Alana.

The court loved the drama and scandal of the tale—an evil, scheming, false son of the king, orchestrating to take the throne and unite Galand and Elamas, who had tried to kill their beloved king and princess. How different the princess was now, and they knew she'd had it in her all along. At least some good had come from the disaster.

If Kinnaird and the others had done their job, no one need ever know that it was the real Alana who had sold her country out to Galand. For what reason, they would probably never know. Much about Alana had died with her. Kinnaird could make up reasons, and most of them would probably be accurate, but Alana had been much smarter about destroying evidence than Gandy.

Who was indeed an agent of Galand and appeared to have worked as a merchant for most of his life, which explained his thorough knowledge of Salhara and its artificial magic. Letters from Pleasant detailed all Gandy had known about the woman he claimed was his 'mother'—a woman that Pleasant had apparently been amorous with as well.

For Alana and her guardian, it would have been all too easy to travel around the country, collecting information and passing it along, arranging all that needed to be done to ravage a kingdom and undermine a king, then deliver all into the hands of the enemy.

At least their attempts at covering up the mess the princess had left behind seemed to be working. The court lapped up the explanations with no real protest. People were frequently as hopeless as they were charming.

Charm turned his thoughts back to Gandy, which reminded him of the madness of the past several days, and he had never been so happy to be home. The only thing he wanted now was to climb into bed and wrap himself around his lover.

Would Reyes be in their bed? Or would he have retreated to his own room without Kinnaird there? Did he still want Kinnaird? It was foolish to think not, there was nothing about Reyes's being a prince that would cause him to end things, and Reyes had said he had accepted he would have had to tell one person his secret, and that had to be Kinnaird.

But Reyes had barely looked at him the entire time they were in the king's chambers that night, and minus the briefest of glimpses of each other before Kinnaird had gone off to do his part in collecting more information and setting lies in place, they'd had no opportunity to see each other. Surely that allowed for wild, paranoid thoughts.

Yawning again, forcing his feet to move because he refused to slip on this most important matter, he finally reached Reyes's office. Shifting the flowers in his arms again, he opened the door and slipped inside, then headed for Reyes's desk—and stopped short in surprise as he saw Reyes already there.

Fast asleep, head pillowed on his arms, hair loose rather than severely braided back… and as he got closer, Kinnaird saw how casually Reyes was dressed. His jacket had been carefully draped across the back of his chair, and the buttons of his shirt were loose, the sleeves rolled up, glasses resting atop of a stack of papers. Kinnaird smiled faintly at the obvious picture— unable to sleep, Reyes had gotten up, dressed, and decided to get some work done. That was Reyes. When in doubt, there was always work to do.

Wanting to touch, but reluctant to wake him up, Kinnaird instead carefully set down the bundle in his arms. Picking up the week-old bouquet of flowers, he set it outside for the servants to take away and then returned to the desk. He carefully cut away the protective paper wrapped around the new bouquet. Orchids, in a bright rainbow of cheerful colors in a crystal vase cut to catch the light and reflect a rainbow all its own.

Setting the vase in the corner where Reyes had always kept his flowers, no matter how the rest of the desk changed, he fussed with them until they seemed as close to perfect as he could manage.

"You clod," said a soft, groggy voice, and Kinnaird jerked in surprise, then smiled ruefully at himself, but he could not think of anything to say, too caught up in staring at his sorely missed lover.

"You are going to beggar yourself buying me

flowers," Reyes continued, sitting up, raking his hair back and rubbing tiredly at his eyes.

Kinnaird smiled. "Then I shall have to obtain gainful employment at the flower house and work for your flowers instead."

"Clod," Reyes repeated, but even at his sharpest, there was no mistaking that word for anything but an endearment.

"You should be abed," Kinnaird said, and moved around the desk, gently taking Reyes's arms and hauling him to his feet. He had only meant to pull Reyes up, then point him toward the door, but once he had Reyes that close, it was as natural as breathing to keep pulling until Reyes was against his chest, in his arms, and the hard knot in his chest finally begin to ease.

"You're not mad," Reyes said, the words muffled against Kinnaird's chest.

"Hmm?" Kinnaird asked, frowning, confused. "Why ever would I be mad? About what?"

"That I lied. That I did not tell you. That I… I'm not who you thought."

"Ah," Kinnaird said, and he supposed it should have occurred to him that Reyes might think him angry. "Why would I be angry? Perhaps a trifle put out that if you had told me sooner we might have been together longer, but I have you now. That is all that matters there. Otherwise, my life is secrets, my dear. I have many of my own, kept for king and country. We have spent the past several days working out how best to lie to an entire kingdom. Besides, it is obviously something that you were instructed your entire life to keep secret, and you did it with the best of intentions. A secret meant to hurt, that would have been one thing. All that aside…" He tucked one finger beneath Reyes's chin and tilted his head up. "You said you had accepted that one person would have to know. I believe you meant me. That you were finally willing to share it, and trust me with it, is all that matters to me."

Reyes relaxed against him, resting his head against Kinnaird's chest, hands tight where they clung to Kinnaird's jacket at his back. "I cannot believe you wake up this early to get my flowers. You really are quite hopeless."

"So long as you love me despite that," Kinnaird said with a teasing smile.

"For it," Reyes muttered.

"What?"

"I said, for it," Reyes said more clearly, looking up at him. "Not in spite of. For."

Kinnaird smiled, too happy to contain it, and bent to take Reyes's mouth in a slow, soft kiss. The last of the knot in his chest eased and faded away, and he shifted to loop his arms around Reyes's shoulders, holding him as close as he could possibly manage.

He was far too exhausted to take Reyes to bed and do all that he would like after so many days apart, but for the time being, the kisses would definitely suffice.

It was Reyes who broke the kiss, drawing back to smile, mussed, flushed, and wet-lipped. "I'm glad you're home."

"Me too," Kinnaird said, stroking Reyes's cheek, his hair. He hesitated, lingering on the dark strands, then asked, "Could I see?"

Reyes looked confused for a moment, then gave one of his soft sighs. "Fine, but you will have to help me fix it. Dying my hair is a damned nuisance, even if I have been doing it all my life."

"Of course," Kinnaird replied, then lifted his hands to sift them through Reyes's hair, summoning up a water-based spell to banish the dye. "I truly cannot believe I missed it. I cannot count the number of disguises I have seen through over the years, and not once did I ever suspect you were wearing one. When I realized it in His Majesty's room..." He shook his head at the memory, still too stunned to form words.

Reyes had bolted, the most afraid Kinnaird had ever seen him, so driven by panic Kinnaird had barely caught up to him. He had followed Reyes inside, only seconds behind him, arriving just in time to see Reyes stand and attack the others, and there had been no mistaking that terrible, destructive force that was the unique magic of the crown. Only then had he seen what had been right in front of his face. By that point, the dripping dye used to hide Reyes's distinctive gold hair had been completely superfluous. When he had struck out to save Rhoten he had looked *exactly* like his father in his younger days.

"People see what they expect to see," Reyes replied, mouth quirking. "My only fears were that you would hate my keeping such a secret from you and that you would no longer find me appealing."

"I am used to the dark hair," Kinnaird mused, "but there is something winsome about you with a royal gold head."

"Winsome?" Reyes echoed scathingly.

Kinnaird soothed his temper with a kiss, nibbling and sucking at his bottom lip before finally drawing far enough away to say, "Gold can be your bedroom hair. I rather like the idea that no one but me will ever see you this way. Well, I suppose I should permit your father to see my secret prince from time to time—" He broke off laughing as Reyes pinched him. "Do not abuse me; I am too tired to properly retaliate. Shall we to bed? I've wanted nothing more than to curl up with you and sleep for days."

Reyes made a low, moaning, whimpering sound

and burrowed into him. "I have scarcely slept these past few days between helping Sharla, pouring over paperwork, helping Father, and missing you—" He yawned suddenly. "Bed sounds wonderful, but I am due to be here in the office in two hours—less now—so there scarcely seems to be any point."

Kinnaird kissed him again. "Can you not rearrange things?"

"No, we are to meet with delegates from Galand to 'discuss recent events' as they so charmingly put it."

"Meaning, certain parties in Galand were not amused to receive Gandy's head and all the incriminating papers from his room that he was foolish not to destroy."

"Precisely," Reyes replied. "They are insisting the trouble was caused by 'independent parties' and 'the Galand throne had nothing whatsoever to do with these heinous acts.'"

"Of course," Kinnaird murmured. "Am I allowed to attend this meeting?"

"Of course," Reyes said, smiling as he echoed Kinnaird. "I did not know you would return so soon, or I would have added your name to the list of attendees."

Kinnaird chuckled at the mild reprove in his tone and kissed his cheek. "Nor I until the last moment, and then I thought I would surprise you—except the full effect of it was thwarted because someone did not have the decency to go to bed and instead fell asleep at his desk."

Reyes smiled and reached up to grasp Kinnaird's face between his hands, then dragged him down for a kiss that *really* made Kinnaird wish he were not so damned tired.

"My dear, you really must stop tempting me, or I shall give in and then embarrass myself for life by passing out at a most importune moment."

"You're ridiculous," Reyes said, laughing, shaking with it as he leaned into Kinnaird again.

Kinnaird kissed the top of his head. "Are you quite certain there is no time to catch a bit of rest?"

"Not for me," Reyes said, not bothering to move from his position cuddled against Kinnaird, eyes closed. "But you do not *need* to attend the meeting with the delegates. You are home two days early. Use that to your advantage and go sleep."

"I will not sleep well without you beside me."

"You're a liar and a fool. We have not been sharing a bed but a few days."

"Which is why you have been sleeping so well?" Kinnaird challenged, not quite able to keep all the smugness from his voice. "Ow!" He started to rub the spot Reyes had pinched, then realized that would require letting go of Reyes.

He did draw back enough to steal one last, long, lingering kiss. "Well, if we are not to be permitted to sleep, order us up some strong coffee and a good breakfast, and we will stay awake by discussing all the things we will do when we take a two week holiday at Keyes Manor."

Reyes pulled away and went to ring for a servant. He was frowning as he returned. "My hair."

"I can do it with magic for now," Kinnaird said, "and you can teach me to dye it properly later." So saying, he reached up and carded his hands through Reyes's hair again, carefully casting the spell until Reyes's more usual color was restored.

Hair fixed, Reyes braided it quickly, tying it off with a pale green ribbon. Then he picked up his jacket from the back of his chair and smoothed the pale green velvet into place, adjusting every last silver button, twitching cream lace until it settled just so. Last, he picked up his gold-rimmed spectacles and settled them on his nose, and no trace of sleepy prince remained, only the secretary Kinnaird had first seen and loved.

He picked up his portfolio and quill and flipped to an appointment page still largely free of obligations. "Two weeks holiday, Your Grace? I think that can be arranged for three weeks hence. Does that fit with your schedule?"

"Perfectly," Kinnaird said with a smile.

"Then I shall mark it in and inform His Majesty. Please make proper note and inform me at once if any changes must be made."

"Of course," Kinnaird said.. "Thank you, Master O'Bannon."

"My pleasure, Your Grace."

Fin

Bonus Shorts

One

If Reyes saw one. More. Flower. He was going to start killing people. Huffing out an irritated breath, he gingerly made his way through the veritable forest of flowers that filled his office, their combined scents strong enough to start a headache buzzing.

There was nothing quite as aggravating as the Days of Devotion, and if Reyes knew a way to go back in time to murder the monarchs who had started the ridiculous three-day-long tradition of giving flowers and other gifts to loved ones, he would do so gladly.

As near as he could tell, 'devotion' was just another word for 'attempt to suck up to the king'. As if it were that easy to do. Reyes sneered at a particularly opulent arrangement of white and yellow roses, unimpressed by the bracelet twined around the gold ribbon securing them.

More bouquets than he could count filled the office, having been delivered steadily throughout the day. Some simply had names on the tags, some had 'charming' little notes, still others bore poetry that made Reyes feel very sorry for the poet.

He carefully pushed aside a dark blue vase holding yellow orchids and a tall stand holding a truly repulsive number of lilies. Did no one understand subtlety?

Finally reaching his desk, Reyes cleared it of the half-dozen vases of flowers piled on it, and then sat down with another sigh. He pulled off his glasses and rubbed at his eyes, wishing he could just retreat for the day and go hide somewhere.

But a holiday did not mean the work stopped, even if it meant everyone tried to pretend otherwise. Rhoten would be mired in meetings and dinners and other celebratory affairs all day long and well into the night—far longer than anyone should force Rhoten to stay up, but hopefully Sharla and Dilane would take care of that.

His task was to catch up on paperwork, and then discreetly start getting rid of the ridiculous flower arrangements overtaking his office. He scowled at the purple vase filled with peonies sitting on the bookcase immediately to the right of his desk.

Did no one realize that flowers given so crassly should not be given at all? Was there a single damned arrangement anywhere in there that was sincerely meant? Reyes made a face and went to pull out fresh sheets of paper to begin drafting a letter to the Krian Emperor. Rhoten would want to look it over before he went to sleep and fuss over it in the morning.

When he opened his desk drawer, however, he found something in it that did not belong: a small package wrapped in orange tissue paper and bound with an orange hair ribbon. Curious and amused, Reyes picked the package up and closed the drawer, paper forgotten. Removing the ribbon, he used it to replace the more demure brown one in his hair.

Pulling away the paper, Reyes lifted one brow as he stared at the velvet jewelry box in his hands. If Kinnaird was giving him a ring, Reyes was never speaking to him again. Opening the box, he smiled to see the tiger lily lapel pin inside. Extracting it, he pinned it to his dark brown, velvet jacket, admiring the detail that had been put into it.

He wondered when Kinnaird would bother to show. Shortly after waking him up in very delightful fashion, Kinnaird had slipped away and not been seen since. Reyes rolled his eyes again, and finally retrieved the paper he had been after in the first place. Setting it on the desk, he opened the drawer that held all his inks and pens and saw yet another package, wrapped in green tissue paper this time. The shape was peculiar, and when he picked it up Reyes realized what it must be. Unwrapping it proved him correct: a bottle of cologne he had admired, but refused to let Kinnaird buy because it was stupidly expensive.

Honestly, he should have anticipated that.

Shaking his head, Reyes set the bottle on a corner of his desk with the few other personal belongings he kept there now because of Kinnaird. Retrieving his ink and pens, he set those on the desk as well, and then opened the drawer where his wax and seals were stored. He was completely unsurprised to see yet another package, this one wrapped in blue tissue paper.

It was large, square, and left Reyes puzzled. Closing the drawer, he set the package on his blotter and slowly pulled away the paper. The velvet jewel box within matched the one that had contained his pin, and he was ignoring for the moment that it was from the most expensive jeweler in the kingdom. Sighing, excited and annoyed all at once, he finally opened the box.

He stared at the contents, and then reluctantly smiled and extracted the beautiful pocket watch. It was silver, etched all over the back and front with tiger lilies. Opening it, he immediately saw the engraving on the inside of the front piece.

*~To my prince
Love, K~*

"Clod," Reyes said softly, and tucked the watch away in the pocket of his waistcoat, attaching the chain to a buttonhole. Where was Kinnaird?

Giving up all attempts at getting work done even though he knew he was going to regret it in the morning, Reyes put back all the things he had taken out, tidied up his desk and put out the lamps. Casting the overabundance of flowers a last scathing look, he left the office, locking it behind him.

He lingered in the hallway right outside the office, worrying his lip as he tried to determine where Kinnaird might have been hiding—and what else he was plotting. There was also the matter of his own gift.

Well, best to start where they had begun, because their rooms were the only place no one was foolish enough to bother them except in an emergency. Walking through the halls, mostly ignoring the people he passed, Reyes went quickly up the stairs and then down the hall towards the suite of rooms allotted to Kinnaird—their rooms, really, since Reyes could not remember the last time he had been anywhere near his own little room at the opposite end of the palace.

The smells of a fine meal struck him first, followed almost immediately by Kinnaird's warm, spicy cologne. The room was dim, with only a few candles offering light, just enough to see the lavish dinner arranged on the table before the fire.

Movement caught the corner of his eye, and he turned in time to go easily into Kinnaird's arms, returning his heated kiss full measure. "Where have you been all day?" he asked when they finally pulled apart.

"Ensuring that we are not disturbed for the rest of

the night and all of the morning," Kinnaird replied, reaching up to tug away the ribbon binding back Reyes' hair and casting a spell that banished the dye in it to reveal its true royal gold color. "I wanted to be able to enjoy my winsome prince at my leisure. Did you get enough work done to keep from fretting about it?"

"It will keep," Reyes said. As much as he hated to admit it, work was far too easy to push aside where Kinnaird was concerned. "Thank you for the gifts. You're a fool and did not have to go to so much trouble—"

Kinnaird cut him off with a kiss, fingers sliding down Reye's back and curving around to lightly grasp his hips. "No trouble at all, I assure you."

"I thought the lapel pin was going to be a ring, at first."

The words made Kinnaird laugh against his mouth. He stole another quick kiss before stepping back and motioning toward the table. "I know very well how much trouble I would be in if I tried to give you an engagement ring during the Days of Devotion. Come, we should eat dinner before it grows cold. I had them make all your favorites." He took Reyes' hand and turned away to lead him to the table.

Reyes swallowed, refusing to be nervous, and said, "So from the way you are laughing, I guess you do not want the ring that I bought you?"

Kinnaird stopped so abruptly he nearly tripped over his own feet and whipped around to stare in surprise. "The what you bought me?"

The nervousness Reyes hadn't been feeling vanished. He clasped his hands behind his back and shrugged. "Nothing of interest to you, clearly."

"Oh, it's of interest," Kinnaird said, narrowing his eyes. He closed the small space between them, standing over Reyes in that way that never failed to make Reyes shiver. "I want my present."

Reyes smirked. "I don't think you deserve it, Your Grace. You laughed at the idea."

Kinnaird grabbed his shoulders and shook him. "You're a brat. Give it to me."

It was only the uncharacteristic anxiety he could see behind Kinnaird's playfulness that finally made him relent. Reaching into his jacket, Reyes extracted the small jewelry box he had kept hidden in Rhoten's desk for the past month, waiting for the Days of Devotion.

He might roll his eyes at the ridiculousness of it all, but Kinnaird was nothing if not a completely hopeless romantic who liked all the nonsense.

Kinnaird took the box and broke into the prettiest smile Reyes had ever seen as he looked at the engagement ring inside. It wasn't anything fancy. The single, small, square cut yellow diamond set in gold had taken him months to save up for, even on his overgenerous salary.

When Kinnaird continued to say nothing, and only stared, Reyes started to get nervous again. "I know it's nothing like what you—" He broke with a muffled noise when Kinnaird kissed him hard, left him breathless.

"Here I thought it would take me years yet to convince you to marry me," Kinnaird said, and he slipped the ring onto his finger, holding his hand up to admire it. Reyes smiled, pleased that it looked just as perfect as he had hoped. "Yes, by the way."

Reyes rolled his eyes. "I did not think you were saying no." Reaching out, he tugged Kinnaird close again and leaned up to kiss him. "Dinner smells wonderful, but are you certain it must be eaten now?"

"I think it will still be tolerable cold," Kinnaird murmured.

"Then take me to bed, fiancé," Reyes replied,

laughing fondly at the way that stupid little word lit Kinnaird's face up, and going easily when Kinnaird dragged him into the bedroom.

Two

Sharla tied a knot in her silk robe, then sat down at her vanity.

Months later, she was still waiting for the dream to end. For someone to wake her up, and drag her from bed to deal with dead bodies; angry, desperate lords who had just gambled away their estates; beaten whores, and all the other things that one must endure as a crime lord.

Every once in a while, she felt guilty for so quickly and effortlessly leaving behind that life that should still be hers. She was as much a dreg of society as those she had lorded it over for so long. A babe abandoned by a mother, saved by dumb luck and raised to be a petty thief, only to be captured and sold to a whorehouse.

Only to be all too good at it—good enough to become the favorite of Lord Klair, and to rise in his personal ranks because she was more than just a good fuck. The real tipping point, however, had been the night Lord Klair saw a knife too late—and his killer had seen *her* knife too late.

She was no stranger to hiding bodies and covering matters up.

Still…when she had finally given in and accepted she was miserable, and asked Kinnaird to get her out, not even her wildest imaginings had taken her along this path. If anyone had told her she would become a princess, on a road to someday be the queen…well, she would have laughed it off, or had the speaker beaten for mocking her, but the words would have hurt.

After all, what poor, lonely, forgotten little girl didn't dream of discovering she was a long lost princess, and going to marry a handsome prince? All girls set such frivolous dreams aside eventually, and lived far more realistic, practical lives—like working up through the ranks of theft, whoring, and murder to rule Cassala from the shadows.

No girl actually woke up one day and found frivolous dreams had come true. Yet here she was, sitting in her royal suite in the royal palace, and everyone addressed her as 'Your Highness' and she had just that day been married to a a handsome duke, a veritable prince himself long before he'd married her, and contemplating the one thing she had never thought to be contemplating.

Women in her world did not have children, if they could possibly help it. Her own mother had probably signed her death warrant when she had gotten pregnant and chosen not to get rid of the babe. Sharla had always put her potions first on her list of necessities, ahead of even food. A pregnant woman could not work, and a woman who could not work…

Now, however, she was not a whore. She was not the mysterious Lord of the Cassala Underworld. She was Princess Alana, someday to be Queen Alana. She was expected to have children, not expected to avoid having them.

It…well, it scared her to death. She lied enough to the rest of the world that she had always tried to be ruthlessly honest with herself. Having children scared her, but she kept catching herself smiling, too. A little boy, she occasionally thought, an exact miniature of his father.

Her stomach gave one of its funny little lurches that always happened whenever she thought of Dilane.

Bad enough she was getting caught up in her life as Princess Alana—but to have to admit she might possibly be the slightest bit besotted with her storybook prince, as well...

She looked again at the array of apothecary bottles on her vanity, all made of dark brown, green, or blue glass. The perfect combination to prevent children, or take care of the problem the following morning. It had never occurred to her that someday she would contemplate never using the potions again. Or at least, not for some years, when there were more than enough royal children running about.

The sound of a door opening made her start in her seat, and she half-turned to see Dilane walking toward her, the door connecting their bedchambers open behind him. There went her stomach again, that damnable lurch. Some former lord of the underworld she was, undone by the warm easy smiles and smoky eyes of her handsome husband.

"Wife," Dilane greeted, grinning as he said the word, their marriage only a few hours old. The grin was equal parts man and boy, and she was probably a great fool but she really *did* want a son who would have that same smile.

Dilane leaned against her bed, his intent plain as day, but he obviously was also content to bide his time. He still wore his breeches, stockings, and shirt, but the shirt was more unlaced than not, and she was looking forward to having all the time she wanted to explore him. It had been a long time—too long—since she had actually wanted someone.

"You look pensive," Dilane said. "What

occupies your thoughts, lovely?"

No casual endearment had ever seemed so sweet—so sincere. Honestly, how had *she* come to be here, in this stolen life, with this man wanting her, and facing the decision she faced? She hesitated, but in the end voiced the question, because it was an important matter in her new life, and not her decision alone to make. "How soon are we expected to have children?"

Dilane looked surprised; clearly it was not the question he had expected. "As soon as we want, really. People will expect heirs in a couple of years, I suppose, but there is no rush. Personally, I would say it is milady's prerogative. You are the one who will have to do all the hard work." He smiled, slow and hot, "Though I am more than happy to do my part."

"So gracious," Sharla murmured, mouth tilting up on one side. She glanced at the neat, tidy row of bottles on her vanity again—then on sudden impulse reached out and swept them all off with her arm, smiling in approval at the tinkling sound of shattering glass, the sharp scent of herbs as they landed in the waste basket next to the vanity.

Then she stood, smiling at his confused but indulgent smile, and loosed the knot of her robe as she strode to the bed. Reaching him, she pushed him back down on the bed and climbed atop him. "Then do your duty, husband, and give me a son."

Dilane grabbed her and flipped them, pushing her down into the soft bedding and kissing her hard. "All right, but afterwards I want a little girl."

"I suppose I'll permit it," Sharla replied, and then there was no more talking.

THREE

Reyes nodded and smiled at the guards standing night duty at the king's chambers. "Good evening."

"Evening, Reyes," one of them said. "Her Highness is still inside with him, but he said to let you on through when you arrived."

"Thank you." The second one pulled the door open and Reyes slipped through, the door closing with a muted click behind him.

Across the room, situated before the fire, Rhoten was fussing over a noticeably pregnant Alana—once Sharla, and a better princess than the real one had ever been. It was a saddening thought, but only Alana was to blame for the fact no one would remember her, only the truly remarkable woman who'd claimed her life.

"Reyes!" Rhoten greeted. "Come, you must see, we can feel the babe moving now."

Alana smiled fondly at Rhoten, who was utterly oblivious as he continued to coo over his grandchild. There was talk and betting all over the palace about whether it would be a boy or girl. Her Highness was determined it would be a son, and Reyes believed her. Not even an unborn babe would want to defy or disappoint her.

She caught Reyes's gaze, and they shared a fond smile. As much as she'd come to love Rhoten, she may as well be the real daughter, and Reyes's secret half-sister. Certainly this was all the family he could have ever wanted, though he wished with all of him that his mother could be there as well.

"Hello, Rey," Alana greeted, and it would never cease to amuse him that she was the only one who ever thought to shorten his name the way his mother once had.

"Lana." He kissed her cheek as he reached her. "How are my two favorite people?"

Her eyes glittered. "I don't think your fiancé would be best pleased to hear he's been demoted."

"His Grace could use the dose of humility."

Alana giggled, and Rhoten chuckled as he rose to his full height, kissing the back of Alana's hand before stepping back. "We all know you would call down the moon for our resident falcon. You fool no one, especially since you were the one who bought that ring he shows off whenever anyone holds still long enough."

Reyes' cheeks burned. "I've told him to stop driving everyone mad, but Kinnaird does as he pleases."

"He's sweet. I don't know how a man with such a dark and cynical job retains his soft center, but he does," Alana said.

Reyes gave her a look. "Says the woman who seems to be fitting perfectly into the role of mother."

"The baby isn't out yet," she replied, but looked pleased all the same. "But I shall bid the two of you goodnight, and go before my ridiculous husband comes looking for me." She kissed Reyes's cheeks, then Rhoten's again, and slipped quietly away.

"Has your bedtime tea been delivered?" Reyes asked.

"Yes, ready and waiting. I also picked out a new book to read," Rhoten replied, "but sit, sit. There was something I wanted to discuss with you first."

Apprehension lanced down Reyes's spine. "What's wrong?"

"Nothing is wrong. You'd know sooner than me if something was," Rhoten replied with a soft laugh.

"Sit, son."

The apprehension eased slightly, soothed by the warmth of that simple word, a word he'd never expected to hear again after his mother had died. Yet here was the most powerful man in the kingdom, claiming him as best he could—and would probably claim him far more publicly if Reyes ever so much as hinted that's what he wanted.

It wasn't, though. Contrary to popular thought, not every bastard child of a monarch wanted the throne. All Reyes had ever wanted was to see for himself the man his mother had loved so deeply. He'd gotten that and so much more. He'd never stop being deliriously happy at the life he'd gained.

Once they were seated, and tea had been poured, Rhoten said, "I like to think my daughter and son-in-law are doing quite well in their new roles."

"Yes," Reyes said, back of his neck prickling with dawning realization. "You want to retire."

Rhoten smiled faintly. "You're always in step with me, on the rare occasion you're not ten paces ahead. Yes, I would like to retire. I'm not getting younger, and you're one of the few who know I can barely read anything anymore. My eyesight will only continue to get worse. I'd rather start training them in full now, and abdicate at a time of my choosing, than wait until too late."

"Of course, Father," Reyes said. "I'll start getting everything in order."

"I have every faith, but that's not why I brought it up. After I abdicate, I would like to take you with me, to be my personal attendant, as it were. I thought I would withdraw for a time, give Alana and Dilane time and space to adjust without everybody running to me every time they do things differently." He chuckled. "I thought you and Kinnaird could come with me, maybe be gone several months, even a year. I don't need a personal attendant as such, not really, I have plenty of well-trained staff I know will happily come with me. But I would like to spend more time with you, outside the confines of station and palace life. If you were amenable, of course. It would require giving up your prestigious position here."

Reyes smiled. "Don't worry, my future husband won't mind taking care of me when I no longer have an income. The trick is getting him to *not* spoil me rotten. The prestige of the position was never what mattered to me. I'd love to come with you, and be your assistant. I'd have been devastated if you'd left without me."

"Good." Rhoten said, and patted his hand. "Good." He pushed slowly and stiffly to his feet, and Reyes rose to offer an arm and escort him to his bed chambers. Once Rhoten was settled for the night, Reyes read to him until he drifted off to sleep a short time later.

Closing the book, he fussed with the blankets, extinguished the lights, and let himself out. "He's asleep. Have a peaceful night."

"You too, Reyes," said one of the guards, and with a last wave Reyes returned to his own chambers.

The guard stationed there, something Rhoten had insisted on ever since the debacle with his late daughter, opened the door for him, and murmured a polite greeting that Reyes returned before slipping inside.

The front room was empty, and the lights seemed to be out in Kinnaird's office, which meant he either hadn't returned yet, or he was waiting in the bedroom.

To Reyes' delight, it proved to be the latter. "Already done causing mischief for the night? Or did you get thrown out for pestering everyone about our wedding?"

"These things take time and preparation," Kinnaird replied huffily. "I want everything to be perfect."

"Everyone knows what they're doing; they don't need you driving them mad," Reyes said, shrugging out of his clothes and putting everything either neatly away or in a hamper to be taken away for cleaning. Naked, he added more wood to the fire and then crawled into bed, where he was treated to an enthusiastic welcome.

When he could talk again, sweat still cooling on his skin, hair a hopeless tangle, but sated and pleasantly drowsy, Reyes related his conversation with Rhoten.

Kinnaird laughed when he was done.

Reyes poked him in the side. "What's so funny?"

"Did he mention *where* we're going on this little retirement jaunt?"

"No...but there are a few manors around the country, for when the royal family must travel. Does it matter?"

"Oh, it most certainly does, because there is one house that belongs to Rhoten, not the throne. It came to him through his mother, and her mother before her. It's always been passed down from parent to child of choice, rather than being entailed and going to the heir." He smirked.

"No. He's not."

"Oh, he is," Kinnaird said with a laugh. "I'll bet you my entire fortune he's taking you to that house to see if you like it, so he can leave it to you someday. Won't *that* be the scandal of the century, the king's pet secretary inheriting his family home!"

"He can't do that!" Reyes said. "I'll kill him, that is not—"

"Your decision to make." Kinnaird dragged him

into a kiss, until Reyes surrendered and kissed him ardently back, dismay over Rhoten and his ridiculousness channeled into his handsome, even more infuriating fiancé.

When Kinnaird eventually drew back, Reyes repeated, "He can't do that!"

"I'm fairly certain he can do whatever he wants with his property," Kinnaird said, and laughed when Reyes smacked his chest. "What? I think it's sweet, and you must be the only one in our circle who hasn't seen it coming. Even our dear princess already figured it out!"

Reyes groaned, letting his head fall to rest on Kinnaird's chest. "I don't need a house. You have more than enough for a hundred families."

"Not quite that many," Kinnaird replied with a soft chuckle. "That's not the point. The point is that he loves you, and wants an important tradition to carry on through you. He can't give you the world the way he would like; let him have this much."

Reyes swallowed the lump in his throat. "I have more than I could have ever dreamed of; if my mother could see me she would cry from happiness. I don't need a ridiculous house or anything else."

"Neither do most of the inhabitants of this palace, but here we are. Stop fussing and let your father spoil you."

Sighing, Reyes gave up. "Fine. But I'd like to be rewarded for my indulgence."

Kinnaird's eyes gleamed. "As you wish."

About the Author

Megan is a long-time resident of queer romance, and keeps herself busy reading and writing it. She is often accused of fluff and nonsense. When she's not involved in writing, she likes to cook, harass her wife and cats, or watch movies. She loves to hear from readers, and can be found all over the internet.

meganderr.com
patreon.com/meganderr
pillowfort.io/maderr
meganderr.blogspot.com
facebook.com/meganaprilderr
meganaderr@gmail.com
@meganaderr